Dear Gowri,

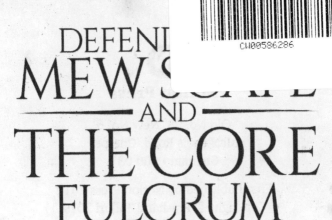

DEFENDING MEW SCAPE
AND
THE CORE FULCRUM

PRASHANTI TALLURI

Best Wishes,

Prashanti Talluri

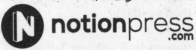

INDIA · SINGAPORE · MALAYSIA

Notion Press

Old No. 38, New No. 6
McNichols Road, Chetpet
Chennai - 600 031

First Published by Notion Press 2019
Copyright © Prashanti Talluri 2019
All Rights Reserved.

ISBN 978-1-64733-595-3

Interior Illustrations by Prashanti Talluri.

Contents

Felidae Aurum

CONTENTS

Acknowledgements

I would like to dedicate this book to my twins Naisha and Nirek. Their enthusiasm and wide-eyed interest in all things bright and beautiful aided me and constantly filled my mind with ideas.

I would also like to thank my spouse Srinivas Talluri for his timely help during the process.

My gratitude goes to my sister, Phani Kumar, for her faith in my abilities. She constantly encouraged me.

Last but not the least, I would like to thank my father, Apparao Yerramilli, who was the rock of my life.

* * *

CHAPTER ONE

School Reopens

Snowball and Goldie were two kittens or you might say -- Cattins because they liked to act much older than they were. Snowball had pure white fur with a little grey on the tip of his tail while Goldie was of golden-ginger colour. They lived in Mew Scape, a little town beside the Purrhy Lake on top of the tallest hillock. Their house was one of the tallest ones in the vicinity, a full six feet in height. Each floor was three feet tall. They were brothers-in-arms most of the time, unless there was a serious cause for disagreement. Today was a special day, as it was the first day of school after summer vacation.

They were going to fifth grade! It sure was exciting!

They jumped out of their comfortable hanging baskets in the second-floor room and ran into the bathroom to brush, bathe, and get ready. Soon they heard their mother holler out from below.

"Fish pancakes coming up on the table. Hurry now Snowball and Goldie before they get cold!"

Goldie's and Snowball's house in Mew Scape

They jumped over each other, slid down the railing, sailed through the air, and landed on the cushioned chairs at the breakfast table.

"WHEE!" they said happily, their eyes dancing.

This did not surprise Niamy, their mother, at all. These two jovial kittens had always been full of energy.

"You have only ten minutes to make it to the bus stop. You don't want to be late on the first day now, do you?"

"Mom, I cannot wait to get to school - to meet my friends again," said Goldie, as he scooped up the fish's tail that was protruding out of the pancake and gulped it down.

"Me too," said Snowball, washing down a piece with a large glass of bat-flavoured milk. "I need to teach Hisky a lesson for pushing me off the bus on the last day."

Hisky was the biggest and meanest grey *kitdent* in the whole of Mew Scape. Everyone addressed kittens studying in school as *kitdents*.

Soon they had finished breakfast and were off, swinging their school bags on their backs. To reach the bus stop, they had to walk down along the winding path to the base of the hillock - next to the Tunnel Garden. They passed several houses as they made it to the base. The other kittens had already assembled. Goldie and Snowball saw five of them. Three of them were familiar while two kindergartners appeared to be new. The two new kittens both had white fur with brown spots. They had cute, bushy tails and looked around nervously. Their parents stood by their side holding their paws.

Kindergartners are so cute, thought Snowball.

These kittens are adorable, thought Goldie. He remembered the time when Snowball and he were also kindergartners. They had come a long way from then.

Amongst those familiar to them, there was Mawny, a female black-and-white second grader. She would cry at the drop of a paw. She smiled shyly when she saw them. There was Ruffoo, a seventh-grader who never brushed his brown fur, and there was Clawcia, their classmate and friend, who always stood up for all her friends. She was a maroon-coloured cat with short, silken fur. They greeted each other excitedly, swishing their tails around; glad to meet after a long summer break.

"Where did you go for your vacation?" asked Clawcia.

"Oh, we went to visit our grandparents at Pausful Isle," said Snowball. "We had so much fun. They thoroughly pampered us."

"We ate and played a lot," said Goldie. "What about you?"

"I went to the Grand Cat Land with my parents, aunt, uncle and cousins! It's the most wonderful place!" she said. "There are so many activities, so many sights and scenes that you will never get bored. I went on the highest and fastest roller coaster. It was scary at first, but once I got used to it, it was a wonderful experience."

All the kittens had interesting stories to narrate about their vacations. Some of them had travelled outside the county, and others had stayed back. A few of them had visiting relatives over, while the others had visited their relatives. Some of them had had an adventurous time, and the others had slumbered peacefully. There were different stories from different families.

The honking and rumbling of an approaching vehicle disturbed their chatting and meowing. It was their school bus. The humongous bus looked like a large mouse and had three floors, two-and-a-half feet tall each, with velvet seats on vertical stands, of which the kittens had occupied around half. The driver of the bus sat on the nose of the mouse; his assistants sat in one ear each and called out to the *kitdents*. Billy, their friend with buck teeth and blue-black fur waved happily at them from his second-floor seat, his bushy tail following suit.

"Hey there, Snow and Gold! I am so glad to see you!" he hollered from the window. They waved back at him.

They shinnied up into the bus using the long, side posts and made their way to seats next to their friends. These buses did not have stairs. Instead, they had scratching posts on the side that served a dual purpose: they helped the kittens sharpen their claws and allowed them to climb the bus. The two kindergartners' parents assisted them into seats at the lowest level. Clawcia, Snowball and Goldie found seats near Billy and starting chatting nineteen to the dozen.

"It is so nice to meet you, Billy! I have missed talking to you. What did you do during your vacation? Did you attend advanced violin lessons as you mentioned you would?" asked Goldie.

"Billy will definitely represent our school during the next Kitaganza event," said Snowball.

Kitaganza was the biennial music and art extravaganza in Mew Scape, with participation from over twenty prestigious schools in the county. Billy could play three different instruments: the keyboard, the violin, and the acoustic guitar. He also liked to sing.

"We did not go anywhere. I stayed back at Mew Scape as I had to assist my father on the poultry farm. The business was booming, and besides, Dad did not have the extra money this time," shrugged Billy.

"Oh, don't worry, Billy. You will soon attend violin lessons. If your father doesn't give you the money, we will find a way," said Clawcia.

"You folks are the best, and I appreciate your offer to help, but I don't want to borrow anything from you right now. I will let you know when the time comes," said Billy.

They continued chatting about other topics, mainly related to the fun times they had spent together in the fourth-grade class. The bus stopped after a while at the last stop, and a large group of kittens jumped onto the second floor. There was a huge uproar where they sat, and a few of the kittens immediately emptied the surrounding seats. It was Hisky, Gattino, Mewtiony, and many other juniors. They were all part of one gang. Many other kittens sat close-by and looked at them nervously. Drawing out his claws, Hisky growled and hissed at them all,

"Empty these seats, all of you! My friends need places. You can find seats for yourselves on other floors."

When the remaining kittens protested, Hisky shoved them out of their seats. Not willing to give up on their precious seats without a fight, those kittens stood up and struck back with their claws. Yowling and screaming, the kittens got into a brawl. Hearing all the noise, the conductor, Ms. Macka, hastily made her way to them.

"No chaos in my bus. No chaos or I will complain to the principal." She separated all the kittens with difficulty and stopped the fight, although her fur looked more dishevelled than before. She scolded Hisky for starting the skirmish. Hisky frowned at her, but kept quiet, and everyone settled down. Snowball chuckled loudly at his expression, causing Hisky to shake a paw at him.

"Mind your own business or I will get you," Hisky whispered while Snowball stuck his tongue out at him.

"No. This time, I will get you," Snowball whispered back at him.

Soon they entered the floating forest, with trees apparently floating over the ground. It was huge, and the bus made its way through until it was in front of a large tree with a trap door. At that point, the bus turned into a live mouse and jumped onto the door that opened up to reveal a tunnel. The mouse started racing through the tunnel, dodging around rocks and bumps. For the kittens inside, it felt like an enjoyable, bumpy horse ride. They giggled as they tossed around and held paws to stay in their seats. The mouse bus scampered along until a bright light was visible at the other end. Cats that inhabited the tunnel in their colourful, brightly lit homes waved at the *kitdents* from their balconies and the *kitdents* waved back. The tunnel was a shortcut that avoided any traffic jams that plagued the thoroughfares during rush hour.

Shortly, they emerged at the other end and what a sight it was! Meow Wow High School was very high and looked like a clowder of cats in different poses. Some were reading books, some running, others thinking, and the remaining in deep discussion. All the cat-shaped classrooms sat on top of cat-post-like dynamic pillars. The school changed its size and orientation every day and sometimes, multiple times a day. Some classrooms collapsed and others rose from below to make way for new lessons. They also rotated around so that the view from each window was ever changing. There was also a special spherical detention room known as the Marble room, which tossed *kitdents* around in it just like marbles. Though the detention room sounded like a fun place to be in, most of them liked to avoid it. An enormous garden surrounded the school with all the sports fields and stadiums behind it.

The mouse bus stopped next to the cheese bus in the large parking zone. The bug, bat and fish buses had already arrived, each making their way through routes most natural to them. The fish bus was water-tight as it had to plunge itself in the river like a submarine. The llama and elephant buses sauntered along the entrance pathway, carrying a large load of kittens. No one wanted to walk in front of either the elephant or the llama bus.

The llama bus spat at anyone that obstructed its way and the elephant bus lifted them high in the air and dropped them on treetops. As soon as the twenty-one buses parked in the parking zone, they turned back into their metallic versions. Many parents had also arrived in their own vehicles to drop their kids. The little ones jumped out of their buses and vehicles, still chatting excitedly. Since Meow Wow High School was one of the most popular schools of the county, one could find practically every type of kitten studying there. Kittens of every shape, size, colour, and fur type walked around the premises. They belonged to both rich and poor families, and the school offered them an inclusive and holistic environment to study. The school also had the reputation of achieving the best standards in academics and extracurricular activities.

Goldie exclaimed when he saw his fifth-grade classroom high in the centre of the school buildings. It was a brown-coloured, bespectacled, cat-shaped room with a rainbow-coloured bow. The name of the classroom was Waffles.

"Yum, named after one of my favourite breakfasts," said Billy.

"Wow, sure looks like a lovely class to be in!" Goldie gushed.

"Can't wait to meet our class teacher and other classmates," said Billy.

Clawcia and Snowball nodded and purred in agreement and their eyes danced at the sight.

They darted on all fours towards the school building and jumped onto the cat posts rising from and falling to the ground. The posts looked like open wooden elevators with large gaps between them, but those gaps were nothing for these agile kittens. They jumped from one moving post to another, never losing their balance until they were on the post moving up to their classroom. Below them, Hisky and his gang also jumped onto the open elevators. Unfortunately, Hisky, Mewtiony and Gattino were also fifth-graders and would be in their class. *How unfortunate!*

There were over fifteen elevators all around the school building to help the *kitdents*. Soon all of them dispersed to their own classrooms, and the fifth-graders stood at a dizzying height in front of the Waffles room. They were at least ten storeys off the ground, each storey being around three feet tall. Green forests surrounded the school on three sides. Little hillocks stood out now and then. Cute little houses and lakes dotted the landscape all around. Tall snow-capped mountains framed the scene to the far-east, and clouds lazily drifted by.

"Ooh," said Clawcia. "What a beautiful scene! We are so high up that even a cat could develop vertigo from here. I have no complaints though. I love it!"

"This is the best view I have ever seen from the school building. We are so lucky," said Snowball.

"What if someone slips and falls?" asked Billy.

"There is no possibility of that. First, we are kittens and second...," Goldie trailed off and pointed behind.

A safe railing ran all the way around the balcony to prevent falls and accidents. The school would not take chances with tiny lives.

"Come on in little kittens, I mean, *kitdents*," said a friendly voice from inside the classroom. They walked in hesitantly, suddenly overcome by a bout of shyness.

* * *

CHAPTER TWO

Fifth-Graders

As they entered through the door, they saw around ten kittens already seated at their cushioned desks. Each desk looked either like a mushroom or a frog. There were five desks in every row, placed on steps that increased in height. A very tall and slender blue Siamese cat sat at the front desk, her sleek tail draped around the chair.

"Meow. Hello and welcome, *kitdents*. I am Professor Neko, your class teacher, and will teach you Languages and Life Sciences. Please take your seats... um... desks," she said.

Hisky and his gang pushed their way through to take the last row of seats. Goldie, Snowball, Clawcia and Billy glared at Hisky before occupying the third row of desks. Soon, the kittens occupied most of the seats.

"Well, well, meow!" said Professor Neko, as she sat cross-legged on her large desk and peered into a notebook she was holding with her front paws.

"It is so nice to see a full class! Let us today start with introductions. Tell me your name, your hobbies, and what you did during your summer vacation."

Meow Wow High School buildings

She began calling each kitten to the front. First it was Grimis, a ginger-and-white-coloured, forlorn-looking kitten.

"Hi everyone, my name is Grimis. My hobby is to chase mice during the day and sheep during the night. I find it hard to fall asleep, that's why."

Everyone broke into laughter. Grimis smiled at their reaction before continuing.

"I went to Furrybank with my family during my vacation. We went sailing," he continued.

Next it was Tufty's turn, a silver-grey cat with a messy tuft of hair on his head.

"Hey everyone, my name is Tufty. My hobby is to watch ClueCat --a detective TV show all day! I love solving mysteries."

Hisky interrupted him.

"Pity you have not solved the mystery of who cut-off the fur on your head and created a tuft!" The last benchers sniggered and covered their mouths with their paws.

"Please be quiet!" said Professor Neko. "The next *kitdent* to interrupt will have to leave the class. Go on Tufty."

"During my summer vacation, I was at Mew Scape with my family, and my cousins visited us. We played around the house and solved some puzzles together."

Next it was Melowflues, a mint-coloured, furry kitten with a high pitched, but sweet voice.

"I love singing everywhere I go. I performed in many places during my vacation at Lussian Peak."

The kittens almost completed their introductions when a new one arrived at the door.

"Hello Ma'am, may I come in?" The new kitten was a beige-and-white Persian one.

"You're late! What is the reason?"

"The alligator bus, which I travel in, got stuck in a swamp, and Lily the anaconda coiled herself around it. We got delayed because of the rescue operation." She looked sheepish as she finished.

The news shocked Professor Neko.

"Oh dear, that is a disaster! Please come in. What is your name?"

"My name is Kattie."

"Kattie -- why don't you introduce yourself? Tell us about your hobbies and what you did during your summer holidays."

Kattie stood in the front near the desk and faced the eager class.

"I would be pleased to do so, Ma'am. My name is Kattie, and I have a younger sister named Mirage. She is in the third grade. My hobby is to perform gymnastics."

There was a resounding 'ah' from the class when she said that. She continued.

"During my summer holidays, I visited Cat Surf Town for a special gymnastics summer camp by the beach."

There was applause from everyone. She was new to school and was hoping she would make good friends. Goldie smiled at her as she sat in the second row in front of him, and she smiled back. Hisky stared at both of them, his claws jutting inches away from Goldie's head. He did not want Goldie to be her friend.

After completing the introductions, Professor Neko clapped her hands and addressed the class.

"*Kitdents*, you realise that you are fifth-graders now. The fifth-grade is a stepping stone to high school. From this year, you will have many new subjects. Some of these subjects will be tough. You must focus on each subject and work hard to pass. Please pay attention now while I help you with the time-table." She turned to the board to create a detailed timetable.

They were to have six subjects that year. Languages and Life Sciences, Environmental Studies and Sciences, Hunting and Culinary Studies, Cat Sports, N-Counters and a choice subject. The options for choice subject were:

- Music (Mewsic)
- Fashion, Etiquette and Art
- Curiosity Kills the Cat
- Lineage and Breeds

These new choice subjects intrigued everyone, as they did not have such subjects in the fourth grade. Goldie, Snowball, Kattie and Hisky opted for the Curiosity course, and so did Tufty. They were obviously curious about the course. Clawcia, Billy, Melowflues and Hisky's friend Gattino opted for music. The rest chose either Fashion or Lineage. After they wrote the timetables and chose their optional subjects, it was time to meet the subject teachers. Professor Neko went to the staff room to call them.

The first teacher to enter the classroom was Professor Noteworthy - the music teacher. He was a tall cat with white fur and had strange black markings that looked like musical notes on his body.

"Class, I am looking forward to creating music together. Who amongst you has a flair for *mewsic*?" he asked in a nasal, singsong manner.

Melowflues was the first to put her paw up excitedly, followed by Billy and the others.

"Ah. Good. It is wonderful to see so much interest from the class. We will achieve the highs and lows of the day in my class. Music is the soulful fuel of the soul." He said, as he blissfully closed his eyes and waved his arms in the air like that of a composer. "Many of my *kitdents* have won medals during the Kitaganza. From tomorrow, I will conduct all music classes in the music room located inside the school building."

He took down the names of the *kitdents* who had applied for music classes. Billy, Melowflues and Gattino were very pleased.

Next to enter was the teacher for Environmental Studies and Sciences, a strict-looking, chubby, green cat, with brown ears and brown polka dots all over his body. He sauntered into the classroom.

"Hello fifth graders! I am Professor Ensure and I will ensure that you are sure about all your facts regarding the environment." he said in a baritone, taking in a deep breath.

"Isn't it a wonderful day today? A famous cat once said, fortune favours the brave. However, I say that it's the weather that favours fortune," he said rhetorically. Hisky and Gattino exchanged looks when he said that.

"I will conduct classes once a week in the garden and twice a week in the classroom. We will learn everything about our environment, the weather, and sciences. We will learn to identify all kinds of plants and animals. We will learn which ones are dangerous for us and which ones are beneficial. One must learn the difference to survive and keep the feline order growing." He looked around, expecting some questions.

"Excuse me sir, but pardon my asking, why is your fur so green? I have never seen a cat with fur like yours," asked Hisky - barely containing a smile. Professor Ensure looked at him sharply.

"If you think I have coloured my fur, you're wrong. We are a family of environmentalists, and over generations, we have evolved to... um... merge with the environment," he said dismissively.

The class broke out in laughter.

"SILENCE!" he said loudly, "The next *kitdent* to laugh will spend detention time on my special tree, and believe me, you will not enjoy it." he said looking around. Everyone kept quiet.

"Now that's much better. I am looking forward to teaching you and learning from you in my classes. As you may have understood, I will not tolerate any silliness or disrespect on anyone's part."

Goldie and Snowball looked at each other and shrugged. They got into trouble often because of their boundless energy. They wondered what the special tree was and shuddered. It was probably best avoided.

The third teacher to enter the classroom was Professor Kitwalk - the teacher for Fashion, Etiquette and Art. She had yellow fur, and was thin and tall, with a long golden ponytail on the top of her head.

"Why, hello fifth-graders! You may not take this subject seriously, but let me remind you of its importance. A cat is not a cat without its cat-walk. Without the right presentation and etiquette, you could just be a clumsy bunny in the wild. Without art, any structure or location would be devoid of meaning and colour. You need art, balance, grace and poise to succeed. I will be your guru for that." She said with a flourish, fluttering her lashes at the ceiling. "We appoint the head Cat and Tom for both academic excellence and these other qualities. It's a pity it's only an optional subject. If I were principal, I would make it mandatory. The Kitaganza is a good platform to showcase what we learn in this class."

Clawcia, Grimis, and Pompom immediately signed up for this class. Pompom had shocking-pink fur, with a bushy tail that looked like a pompom. Goldie fidgeted in his seat when he imagined himself cat-walking down the hallway in front of the principal. He was glad it was an optional subject. He had two left feet.

Clawcia however was open to making it a mandatory subject. She believed art and poise were the answers to every cat's dream. According to her, every successful cat had to have good etiquette.

"I will conduct the classes in the school's large art room, next to the scratching-post room," said Professor Kitwalk.

Coach Dudgeble was the next teacher-a cat who had a brown body, but black limbs. His middle was as round as a basketball, but he had rather muscular arms and legs. He blew a whistle as soon as he entered, and all the kittens automatically stood up.

"Well, well. What a class, what a class. Please take your seats," he gestured with his arms, and everyone sat down. He put one of his arms up with the index toe pointing up.

"This school has produced great *kitdents*, and they have made us proud. They have excelled in sports, and we have always been in the top three teams of the annual global Catalympics. Yes, they have made Meow Wow and Mew Scape proud, and I can see that you will do us proud too. We will embark together on this wonderful journey of mastering all sports and winning the crown this year -- especially for Kitdart -- the obstacle team-game of skill, stealth and strength. Training for it begins in fifth grade, and I am hoping the best player is from this class."

Everyone knew about Kitdart, had watched it as a part of the audience, but had never played it before. It was a senior's sport, a very dangerous game, but highly popular. It tested the notion of cats and their nine lives. Snowball remembered how badly one senior got injured the previous year while playing, because of which they took him to hospital. Despite its dangers, everyone wanted to learn and excel in the game because of the prestige attached to it. Meow Wow school had won the silver medal last year in the Catalympics, having lost to Great Skats school only by one point.

The last teacher for that day was Professor Inabaox, for the 'Curiosity Kills the Cat' subject. Everyone had been waiting for more information about this class. He was a squat, purple-coloured cat, who wore a blue robe and had long black whiskers. His large blue eyes behind horn-rimmed glasses looked ominous but intellectual.

"Dear fellow detectives...", he started. "I must warn you at the outset. This is the first time we are conducting this training for your class, as we thought it was a necessity."

Everyone sat upright when he said that. *What did he mean by it was a necessity?*

"After an unfortunate event, we thought we needed help from many brave cats and kittens to deal with such unforeseen catastrophes. I shall discuss the details of which with the *kitdents* in the first class. With this training, I shall equip you to join us in solving this and other mysteries that have been plaguing us. If you drop out because of fear, you may do so before your oath taking ceremony. This class um... may include some peril; however, don't worry. The seniors will protect you."

Snowball, Goldie, Kattie, Hisky and the rest of the class closed their mouths, which had opened and exchanged a few glances. *What on earth were they getting into? They could not back out now.* Snowball was the first to speak.

"It will be an honour for us to be part of this class, sir. There is no question of dropping out now." He placed his paw on his heart.

Goldie, Kattie and Hisky also agreed. The other kittens seconded their opinion.

"That's good. I cannot wait to start with the new batch," said the professor.

The other three teachers were not available that day for an introduction. However, Professor Neko mentioned that they were: Professor Piquant for Hunting and Culinary Studies, Professor Manimore for N-Counters and Professor Hisstoly for Lineage and Breeds. It had been a whirlwind of a day. When the school bell rang at three o'clock, all of them started queuing up to board their buses, which waited for them in the school grounds. Kattie stopped in front of Goldie.

"Hi, it was nice to meet you today. I did not get your name?" she extended her paw.

"I am Goldie and this is my brother Snowball. Also, these are my friends Billy and Clawcia." They shook paws with each other.

"Nice to meet you Kattie," they said, smiling.

Kattie was glad to make new friends. It made school so much more interesting.

"Glad to meet you. I hope you don't mind if I hang around with you?"

"Not at all. You are most welcome," said Goldie.

Hisky interrupted from behind.

"Hi Kattie. A kitten like you should not hang around with them. These cats are losers. If you want company, be with us. We are the most intelligent bunch and the strongest, too."

"Yeah we are," said Gattino.

"The best and the bravest bunch," said Mewtiony.

Kattie turned around shocked to see Hisky grinning from ear to ear at her. Gattino and Mewtiony stood behind him.

Snowball glared at Hisky.

"Be quiet, Hisky! Everyone knows that you get into trouble the most! Leave Kattie alone. She is our friend now."

Hisky raised his paw to punch Snowball, and Snowball raised his.

"How dare you interrupt me, Snowball! I will teach you a lesson." He took a swipe at Snowball, who stopped him with his fist.

Goldie and Billy pushed them apart.

"Stop it -- you two. You are attracting needless attention." Hisky's ears turned scarlet with suppressed aggression.

Professor Neko - who was chaperoning the kittens out, turned around at the commotion.

"What's going on there? Everyone be silent and join your own bus queues please."

"I will see you tomorrow," said Kattie to Clawcia -- totally ignoring Hisky and walked towards the alligator bus queue.

Hisky and Snowball continued glaring at each other for some time.

As they passed the principal's grand office, Goldie saw Professor Inabaox seated in front of the principal -- Professor Quemarke, deeply engaged in conversation with him. The principal, an orange-and-black striped cat, was actually a half-breed Lynx. His sharp eyes and ears turned towards the door just as Professor Inabaox urgently said,

"We have got to find it, Professor Quemarke, or we will all be in danger. It will lead to our destruction."

He stopped Professor Inabaox mid-sentence, gesturing him to shut the door - who got up and shut the door behind him, sound-proofing the room.

Goldie, curious about the conversation, would ask the professor during the first class. Something was up in the usually safe school and he wanted to find out. The kittens approached the gigantic central corridor to descend using the two large elevators decorated to look like carousels. The elevators descended while rotating so they could occupy empty seats from any side. Soon they reached the ground-floor - having thoroughly enjoyed their carousel ride and ran towards their school buses.

That night, Goldie could not sleep well and looked at Snowball fast asleep in the hanging basket next to his. Professor Inabaox's comments kept ringing in his mind. He had to investigate the mystery. Still immersed in his thoughts, he looked out of the open window, at the full moon lighting up the room and surroundings. Out of view, a worm buggy glided on the grass noiselessly carrying a passenger towards the docks of Purrhy lake where a swan-shaped boat lay waiting. A cloaked individual exited the worm buggy to board the swan boat. On board the boat, another cloaked being--presumably the captain, shook paws and handed over a map to the first one.

* * *

CHAPTER THREE

The Crystal Cavern

The next day, when their bus reached school, the configuration of the classrooms had completely changed, and the fifth graders followed the hovering wasps--holding directions, to the rear of the building. Their classroom was on the ground floor today. Kattie saw Snowball and ran over to join him in front of the class. In the sky overhead, they could see the eagle and parrot buses circling around--to find a place to land in the school ground. Once everyone assembled, the first teacher walked in. It was Professor Piquant. She looked like a furry, red-coloured, erinaceous rambutan (a tropical fruit), with the legs of a cheetah. The legs were yellow-coloured with black and dark-brown spots.

"Hi class! Welcome to the first class on Hunting and Culinary Adventures. I am Professor Piquant. We will get started on something interesting right after all the introductions."

Once they completed all the introductions, she resumed.

"Today we will hunt dangerous Grotiders for a delicious golden soup. Follow me into the prickly grove for this lesson. Please ensure to sharpen your claws before every hunting expedition."

Kittens with blunt claws sharpened them using the scratching posts scattered around school. After that, they followed her in a single file, out of the building, into the open assembly area, to board wormlike buggies, each of which could hold ten *kitdents*. The antennae of the worms quivered in the air. When they all settled down, the buggies started sliding like millipedes weaving and gliding smoothly on scores of tiny legs.

Melowflues burst out laughing as she felt tickled all over. Almost everyone followed up with guffaws of their own. Off they went quickly, a giggling-clowder of cute little kittens. They passed the huge outdoor stadium on their way through the rear gates. The buggies had the ability to climb vertically also, as the kittens found out, when they reached the grove. The grove was on the outskirts of school and contained large trees that resembled prickly palms. These palms had poisonous spines that caused bad rashes and fevers. The kittens kept their paws inside for safety and tightened the seat belts around their abdomens. The buggies vertically climbed a large palm tree, with the kittens holding on for dear life. They then glided over the canopy of palm leaves, bobbing up and down, before descending the trunk of a large palm near a clearing. When they reached the clearing in the grove's centre, they stopped.

"All *kitdents* assemble in the centre and touch nothing," said Professor Piquant. "We have to be silent. These Grotiders live in burrows below these palms and are a big menace. They will eat anything, even fur." Everyone felt apprehensive when she mentioned that.

She held out a picture of a Grotider. It was a large mustard-coloured rodent, with eight legs. It had a long

The picture of a dangerous Grotider

snout, black-beady eyes and four, long, curved teeth: two each on the top and bottom of its jaw. Its ears were circular, and its tail was long and thin, with a bushy ball of fur at the end.

It looks so queer, like a mix between a mouse, a baboon, a spider and a toy, thought Snowball.

"The meat, prized, makes for a tasty treat," continued Professor Piquant. "The technique to catch a Grotider is to ambush it and surround it from all four sides. When you do that, it will curl itself into the shape of a ball. At that point, you grab it and throw it into this basket. If you leave any space, it will escape not to emerge from its burrow again till the end of the day." Showing everyone the basket for collecting the Grotiders, she got down on all fours into the stalking position and showed them how to wriggle their backs before lunging forward. All the kittens practised the technique and helped each other. Soon they were ready. At that point, she led them towards a large palm tree with a big burrow opening below it. "Goldie, Hisky, here, take these sticks and tap the trunk. The others -- crouch and wait until one emerges."

Hisky and Goldie took the sticks reluctantly and gently started tapping the trunk -- careful to avoid the spikes. Soon, they heard a long, loud squeak, and a big Grotider emerged from the burrow. Hisky and Goldie lunged at it from one side, while Billy and Melowflues blocked its escape route. The Grotider tried escaping, but the kittens surrounded it, not allowing it to find any gap between their feet. Finally, after a few minutes, feeling trapped, it halted in its tracks and rolled up into a ball. Goldie grabbed it, placed it in the basket, and securely locked the lid. Similarly, the other kittens formed groups of four and caught four other Grotiders. During the last such catch, Tufty scraped his paw against a spike and yowled in pain. The result was almost instantaneous --his paw started turning blood-red and swelling up. The Grotider took advantage of the situation and escaped.

"Oh-oh. I have some antidote. Here, let me treat your paw--you will feel better," Professor Piquant said and applied the medicine to Tufty's paw. Tufty's face took on a green shade, and his stomach felt queasy. The professor asked him to rest in the buggy.

Having collected five Grotiders, Professor Piquant was happy to lead them to the kitchen on the right of the school buildings, to teach them how to make soup. A nurse took Tufty to the sickroom to stay under observation. His face had turned entirely green by then. The others headed to the kitchen pond and garden to collect the other ingredients. They collected tender basil leaves and fished out some grass carp from the pond. After heading into the open kitchen, everyone put on aprons and gathered around four large cauldrons. Snowball, Goldie, Kattie, Clawcia, and Billy shared one cauldron. Similarly, the others formed groups to share cauldrons.

After twenty minutes, the lesson was complete, with steaming-hot, golden soup boiling in four large cauldrons. They tasted a spoonful of the soup from each cauldron to check the flavour. Clawcia felt the soup they made tasted perfect. Professor Piquant would distribute the soup to everyone in the cafeteria for lunch as a complementary course. The kittens removed their aprons and started heading back to class for the next lesson.

Hisky said to Snowball and Goldie, "The soup you made tasted so bland. She wasted the lesson on you."

Gattino agreed with him. "Yes, you are right Hisky. It tasted insipid."

"It was like watered-down medicine. BLEH, I hate medicine," said Mewtiony. Hisky and Gattino patted him on the shoulder, laughing out loud.

Snowball felt anger rising in him again. Goldie asked him to ignore them.

Clawcia turned to Snowball to comment.

"Don't listen to them. It tasted great."

Kattie and Billy agreed with her.

"My mother makes tasty soup, and this was as delicious as what she makes," Kattie said.

Calming down, Snowball shrugged at Hisky.

"Heard them? It's in the tongues. Too many sour tongues spoil the taste," he said and winked before they sped off -- giggling, leaving Hisky, Mewtiony and Gattino fuming.

The next class was the optional one, so Snowball, Goldie and Kattie walked towards the basement for their first Curiosity class. Tufty had not yet returned from the sickroom. This was the class Goldie had been waiting for. There were so many unanswered questions in his mind, which he was hoping, would get clarified. They jumped onto the moving post that descended into a well-like structure, going deep into a natural cavern below the school. School rules forbid them from descending into this well previously.

The post stopped when they reached the cavern at the bottom. They entered the passcode the professor had given them, and the door opened. What a sight greeted them! The whole cavern was lit up by hanging lanterns and fireflies that reflected a million times in the crystallised ceiling. The kittens gazed around them and at the ceiling in awe. The fireflies flitted around creating the illusion of infinite glimmering sparkles. The professor had asked them to attend classes in a room beyond the Crystal Cavern. They saw a corridor at the end of the enormous cavern and bounded towards it.

"Hello?" Snowball called out, hoping someone would answer, but his own voice echoed back. The silence was deafening in the long corridor. Snowball started getting worried, Kattie's mouth felt dry, and Goldie felt a shiver go down his spine. Their footsteps seemed loud in the silence. At the end of the never-ending corridor, they saw a door and ran towards it. They knocked on the door, and Professor Inabaox immediately opened it.

"Come in," he said, his finger on his mouth. They quietly entered the cave that had multiple stone shelves on its walls and many tunnels opening from it. The school had its own underground cave system! Goldie was not aware of this. There were approximately ten other kittens in the room, and Hisky was amongst them. He made a thumb-down sign when he saw Snowball and Goldie -- who ignored him. It was dimly lit and one of the gloomiest places they had ever seen. They sat on the stone ledge, waiting for the class to begin. When all kittens had arrived, Professor Inabaox began.

"Friends and *kitdents*, today we gather as it's the need of the hour. We are in grave danger as the authentic Core

Fulcrum has disappeared from its hidden spot. We found a note outside the spot mentioning that they would destroy it when they find the Pivot. Time is running out. We have to find the culprit before it's too late and return the Core Fulcrum to its rightful place."

There were gasps from all the *kitdents* in the cave. *The Core Fulcrum had disappeared? The source of balance and magic in the cat world, the heart of any feline's agility and the very reason that cats had nine lives had disappeared? If someone destroyed that dazzling nucleus, they would cease to exist.*

Goldie asked, "Sir, how is that possible? Isn't the Core Fulcrum the most closely guarded object in the world? Only a few cats would be privy to its location."

"Not a few -- only two. One of them is our principal Professor Quemarke. The other is the president of Lussian Peak, President Skailimet. However, because of the circumstances, they took me also into confidence. This is a breach of the highest order. We need a large group of supporters to find the culprits."

"Why fifth-graders?" A squat looking senior *kitdent* with rough looking fur asked. He referred to Goldie and Snowball. "Isn't this task a little too risky and confidential to involve such young kitdents?"

"Ruffsaw, we believe that the enemy is not just one person. We need an army of brave fighters to deal with a large group of enemies. We need as many *kitdents* as possible. Once we retrieve the Core Fulcrum, we will change its location. In addition, we will not recruit all *kitdents* who apply. We will conduct a test for everyone and recruit only the bravest and the quickest *kitdents*."

Satisfied with that explanation, the kittens awaited the instructions for the test. They were excited and apprehensive. Professor Inabaox handed over sheets that contained maps of the underground caverns to each *kitdent*.

"The caverns are the venue for today's session. I will conduct the remaining training sessions either in classrooms or the school-grounds as appropriate. These caverns are deep, extensive and labyrinthine hence these maps are mandatory. They will be your lifelines. If you get stuck, one of the senior assistants will find you with the help of guide bats. However, if any of you suffer from claustrophobia, you must speak up now." he looked around, expecting some disinclination.

As expected, a paw sheepishly went up. It was Purrplex, a purple-and-white-coloured and chubby sixth-grader.

"Sir, I can fight bravely against any enemy in the open, but I choke in closed spaces. Please leave me out of this mission."

"Very well. However, I need your paw-print on the non-disclosure form -- the terms for which I have included in the details. You also need to eat a Valerian stem. This stem's juice will prevent you from speaking about any undisclosable secret, except with others who have consumed it too."

Aha clever. The juice created an enforced club of sorts. I will call it the Curiosity Club, thought Goldie.

Purrplex read the details that included expulsion for failure to comply with the non-disclosure terms and conditions. He added his paw-print at the bottom and ate the Valerian stem. It tasted horribly bitter and contorted his face into a nasty expression as he swallowed it. His cheeks swelled up, his eyes widened, his fur stood on end, and his nose looked like it would slide right off his face. Minutes later, as others watched, he became normal and looked like nothing had happened. Soon he exited the room.

After witnessing what had happened to Purrplex, Hisky started having second-thoughts, but he couldn't bear to depart in front of the Manzar twins: Snowball and Goldie.

The Professor called all *kitdents* forward to imprint their paws on the NDA forms and to provide them with Valerian stems for consumption. They willingly did the former and reluctantly the latter. There were screeches and yowls in the cavern because of the distortions, and then soon everything returned to normal. Snowball almost had a laughing fit when he saw Hisky's eyes and ears droop sideways, but he couldn't laugh as his tongue got elongated and almost dropped out of his mouth. Goldie's tail curled up like a pig's and Kattie's whiskers grew longer than her tail. Everyone reacted to the juice differently, each with an equally hilarious side-effect.

When everyone stopped giggling and completely calmed down, Professor Inabaox addressed the group again.

"Welcome to 'Curiosity Kills the Cat' club, or you may refer to it as the Curiosity Club. This is a subject for which the first two lessons are tests, both of which we will conduct today. The first test is the chase of the fireflies and the second test is an escape from the deep labyrinth. I shall recruit only those *kitdents* who pass both tests." He checked if the *kitdents* had questions. When they didn't, he continued, "For the fireflies' test, we will release three fireflies - two golden ones and one more of another colour. The colour will determine the trait of the firefly. For instance, the blue ones will emit a laser light to confuse and attack you, the green ones will attempt to spit into your eyes, and the red one will throw a dart of fire at you. You must watch out, as it stings a lot. The golden ones are mostly harmless although they can sting sometimes. I will hand you a jar and a net. Catch the fireflies within ten minutes, with the help of the net and trap them in the jars."

A shiver ran down everyone's spines. These did not seem like easy tasks.

"Let us proceed to the underground amphitheatre for the first test."

They walked through the first door in a single file down what seemed like over a hundred rocky steps, and soon they were at the amphitheatre. Ropes hung from the ceiling, between the criss-crossing ledges under it. All the kittens took their places on benches all around and waited for the tests to begin.

It was Kattie's turn first. She took a net and jar and slung them around her neck. She was ready. Professor Inabaox took a blue-black jar, and an assistant put a few ordinary flies in them. The professor took some sparkling dust out of his pocket and sprinkled it in the jar before placing the lid back on. Then, he held the jar and swirled it around three times. Having completed that action, he opened the jar to release the flies. Two golden fireflies and one red one flew out. The kittens watched the process with amazement.

"Here you go Kattie!" yelled Professor Inabaox. "Watch out for the red one which can shoot darts of fire and burn your fur."

Kattie setoff as they started the timer. The fireflies flew to the ceiling, and Kattie jumped from one ledge to another deftly. She could retrieve the two golden ones effortlessly. They buzzed silently in the jar as she put them inside. The red one flew out of sight. Suddenly it appeared above a rope. She jumped and caught the rope below it to climb up as it buzzed and took off again. She plodded on to chase it while everyone cheered her on from below. Suddenly the firefly stopped and turned around to face her.

"Watch out!" said Professor Inabaox as a fire dart blazed out, missing Kattie's ear by a fraction of an inch. Just as the firefly landed on the ceiling, Kattie's net closed around it and she swept it into the jar deftly. Mission accomplished.

Soon the only two kittens remaining were Goldie and Hisky. All but one kitten had passed the test. A seventh grader named Astor had failed the test and had to exit. The blue firefly had emitted a laser beam which had blinded him, and he had fallen from the ceiling onto the carpet below.

Professor Inabaox's assistant handed Hisky the jar and the net. Then he released the three fireflies. They were two golden ones, and a green one. Hisky could have sworn the green one had long fangs. As soon as he released them, they buzzed out of sight. He climbed the ropes and made it to the ceiling to jump onto the top ledge. He suddenly saw them on the opposite side of that ledge. He sprinted as fast as he could and retrieved one golden firefly, which was looking confused. However, the other two disappeared. On separating the curtains attached to the ledge, he located the green one hiding in the folds. Its eyes suddenly became large and letting out a piercing scream spat out in fury. A green, gooey liquid splashed into Hisky's left eye. He lashed out with the net as he lost balance and fell. The green firefly got caught in it. He lost no time in trapping the firefly in the jar. The last one flew below to settle on a stone bench. Though his eye was stinging, Hisky got up and trapped the last firefly also just as the timer rang. He was just in time.

After washing his eyes with the water handed out by the assistant, he was in time to see Goldie meet his match. Everything looked green around him. Goldie had to catch a rainbow-coloured firefly, and this one could shoot lasers, fire darts or spit. He caught the two golden ones almost as soon as the assistant released them by jumping high in the air, but the rainbow one disappeared from sight. He climbed up the ropes like the others to get a good view, but he still could not see it. Just as he was giving up, he saw a spectrum of light from a lamp at the far end of the room and darted towards it. The firefly had settled in front of the lamp. Just as he neared it, the firefly flew to a stone bench below and Goldie lunged after it. The firefly shot a dart of fire that singed his nose, but Goldie caught it anyway. Buzzing irritably, the firefly reluctantly settled into the jar. Goldie had made it! Everyone clapped for him when he returned with the jar, and the assistant gave him medicine for his nose, which had a big blister.

Now it was time for the second test. The twelve remaining *kitdents*, the assistants and Professor Inabaox made their way to the deep labyrinth. They were in a cavern with multiple tunnels leading out of it.

"For this test you can work in groups of twos or threes. Please use the maps we have given you. When we begin, you will make your way through these tunnels and emerge outdoors into the great lawn. You will get twenty minutes. If you do not reach outside within that time limit, you will fail the test."

Kattie, Goldie and Snowball teamed up, and Hisky teamed up with Ruffsaw and Kuting. At the sound of the whistle they were off. Each team entered a different tunnel. Goldie had brought his laser reflector and turned it on to peer over the map. He located entrance nine, the one they had entered and drew a line to the nearest exit through several dozen turns and intersections. It looked like a very difficult maze. Snowball had brought some chalk and a pencil with him. They numbered the intersections with the pencil on the map and numbered them with chalk on the rock.

"Good idea!" said Kattie. "You both are smart."

Having planned the strategy, they were off, rapidly making their way through the labyrinth. In multiple places, they had to crawl through narrow openings, but they worked together as a team and always emerged safely. At each intersection, they marked the numbers on the rocks and circled the corresponding opening on the map. At some places, eerie worms and insects fell on them, but they brushed them off. Some paths were circular, which meant they passed the same tunnel more than once. However, with persistence, soon they heaved themselves up into the open greeted by applause from Professor Inabaox and the assistants. They were the first to arrive.

Hisky and team arrived immediately after them, emerging out of a burrow below the old Peepal tree. The rocks to the exit gave way when they emerged. Ruffsaw had a scorpion walking on his back. It was about to sting when he flicked it away, and it crawled off into the bushes.

"Phew, that was a close shave," said Ruffsaw. Hisky couldn't agree more. He was a little upset that the Manzar twins had emerged before them.

Another team of sixth and seventh graders Pilli, Bekku and Lemeow emerged out of a hollow of a tree at the other end of the lawn. Pilli had an amoeba centipede crawling on her braid. As soon as she screamed in horror, it fell off and slithered away. She was lucky as centipedes are some of the most poisonous arthropods in the world. The group of waiting kittens ran towards them applauding. There was no sign of the last team. After ten more minutes, the assistants ran into the labyrinth to find them with the help of guide bats.

"Alas, you haven't made it," Professor Inabaox informed the last three -- Mewmag, Scratchpad and Cherie, when they arrived. "The remaining nine have made it." he said. Applauding the effort of the nine who had made it Professor Inabaox welcome them officially into the team. "We shall begin training from the next lesson. I congratulate all the winners today. You have fought hard to win."

They cheered and applauded for each other, looking forward to starting the battle against the snipers of the Core Fulcrum.

CHAPTER FOUR

King Koresque

Felidac
Aurum

The passage that led to the secret underground chamber was dark and damp. Water trickled down the sides of the well, as Trixy and Joybob carried the sparkling cube into the moss-covered burrow, just above the waterline. It was a tight squeeze sometimes.

"Watch out!" said Joybob. "We cannot afford to break the cube after all the trouble we've been through!"

"SQUEAK! What do you mean -- we? It's been my effort all along while you watched," said Trixy, his cloak dragging on the floor.

The black sack they had covered the cube with completely tore in the burrow because of the sharp edges around, hence they tossed it out. After that, they jostled along, daintily balancing the cube that was hovering in the air between them. It threw beautiful patterns of light all around in the underground tunnel. Soon they were in the mossy, main chamber and could see shapes bowed and huddled, in front of them. Someone whispered,

"Bow down. King Koresque is arriving!"

Trixy and Joybob joined the milling crowd to genuflect on the wet mossy floor.

"HAIL THE GREAT KING KORESQUE! HAIL THE GREAT KING KORESQUE!" They all said in unison -- raising their heads and bowing again many times.

A large mole-rat bandicoot, wearing a shiny blue armour, a crown, and a large red cloak arrived through a tunnel at the rear of the chamber. A large group of soldier-like mole-rat bandicoots brandishing spears and swords arrived shortly after him. It was King Koresque, the monarch of all the rodents in the world. There was a gasp from the crowd. He was the ugliest mole-rat bandicoot they had ever seen, with a scar running along one cheek. Towering above others, one eye completely hidden by a brown tuft of fur, the other one beadily looking at the crowd, he rasped,

"Where is the Core Fulcrum? I want to see it now."

He sat down on the rocky, large, makeshift throne in the centre of the chamber.

Trixy and Joybob made their way to the front, elbowing their way through the crowd.

"Excuse me, sir. Ma'am, could you please excuse us?"

They carried the cube to the centre, its light dancing magically on the walls and ceiling.

Everyone looked at the cube - mesmerized by its hovering act and its dazzling beauty. No sooner had they carried the cube to the king than he grabbed it and threw it on the floor. The cube did not hit the floor, but gently bounced off some invisible platform and bobbed around for some time before settling down.

"What's this? Why isn't it breaking?" asked the king annoyed at this development. "I want this destroyed. This is the source of all our problems. This cube provides all the agility, balance and other magical abilities to the cats of this world. With that power, they destroy us mole-rats and other rodents. We have no freedom as long as they have this power. If we want to be the superpowers of the world, we must destroy this cube. No cube, no cat power."

"This is the Core Fulcrum your majesty. We cannot destroy the cube without the Pivot," said Joybob.

"I know this is the Core Fulcrum, but what is the Pivot?"

"It is the only object that can weaken this cube and destroy it. We think it's another object that magnetically or optically interacts with this one."

King Koresque grabbed Joybob by his hind legs and dangled him in the air, who started flailing his arms.

"Find this Pivot and destroy the Core Fulcrum, or you will meet your end. Do you understand?"

"Squeak! Yes master!" said Joybob, desperately trying to free himself.

"Keep this cube in the royal dungeon until you find the Pivot. You have two weeks to find it," he flung Joybob into the crowd before sitting on the throne again. Joybob scurried to the rear before the king could catch him again.

Then the team of architects presented the progress of the new underground city called Vamoush, designed to

King Koresque dangled Joybob in the air

be indestructible. This was the king's secret mission. He wanted mole-rat bandicoots to become the most powerful species in the world. Finally, the king reviewed the plans and stood up.

"Although the progress is good, as reviewed, I would like the enemy trap systems to be better. Except for that aspect, everything else looks good. I am looking forward to moving to this new city within the next two weeks. With its secret passages, traps, labyrinths and advanced defence system, we will be unsurpassed. Find the Pivot before we inaugurate the city. Once it is in our control, the destruction of our mortal enemies is imminent. We shall reassemble next week." He waved his hands dismissively. The royal guards took the cube away while everyone dispersed. King Koresque walked away, followed by his soldiers, the red cloak swept behind him.

At school, Snowball was getting distracted during the Languages' class. They were learning different gestures and signs from historical times. He looked outside the window and saw ducks waddling in the pond next to the classroom. The pond also had beautiful pink and white lotuses. Professor Piquant's class was going on in the kitchen next to the pond in the middle of the herb garden. He brought his attention back to the class where a role play was in progress. Hisky was bent before Melowflues.

"Purr...," he said.

"Purr, purr, purr" repeated Professor Neko asking Hisky to bend a little more. "Act very pleased to see the queen," she said.

Melowflues, wearing a cape to imitate a queen, was looking distinctly amused. Everyone giggled. It was priceless to see Hisky bent this way.

"Purr, purr," he tried again, bending his forelegs forward and arching his back, in a mark of greeting and respect.

"Now a confident cat always raises her head and straightens her tail before responding," she told Melowflues.

"Purr, purr. Meow. Welcome to the castle," said Melowflues straightening her tail and looking at Hisky confidently.

"Thank you, your highness. Please accept these gifts from our kingdom," Hisky bent forward until his nose was almost touching his toes.

"Very good role play--*kitdents*. Well done. We have learnt the history of royal cats that lived in this very land a century ago and learned their art of communication." Professor Neko beamed happily as she packed up her files in her bag to leave for her next lesson.

The next class was in the school's botanical garden, filled with bouquets of flowering plants and trees, located to the left of the musical fountains and swimming pool. Professor Ensure was already there - almost camouflaged against the backdrop of green lantanas.

"Ahem!" he cleared his throat and began. "Today we shall learn the importance of Lantana bushes. These are the best refuge for a cat during sunny days, but that is not all. These are not ordinary Lantana flowers. If you look at them closely, you will see the flowers either facing the sun or prey." He released a mouse he was carrying in his satchel, and sure enough, all the green flowers turned to face the mouse, as it darted under a boulder, its whiskers quivering with nervousness. He continued, "If you pluck these flowers, they emit a very high-pitched shriek which other flowers join in to create an unbearable cacophony. When it is about to rain, they droop downwards and when it is about to snow, they shiver while their petals flutter to the ground. Because of these qualities, scientists named them as the weather flowers."

This left everyone astonished. They never knew these simple flowers were so magical.

"I will show you something else interesting about these flowers. Spread out and find as many fallen petals as you can and bring them to me. Be careful not to pluck any of them."

Goldie, Billy and Snowball ran to the next bush to search for the petals. Clawcia and Kattie started gathering petals from the bush the professor was standing next to, as he did not seem to mind. Hisky, Gattino and the rest walked to the other side. Soon they returned, their paws full of petals. Hisky and Gattino exchanged glances rolling their eyes. They were apparently not enjoying the lesson. The professor produced a glass jar out of his bag and asked everyone to drop the petals in it. He then drew a circle in a bare patch and placed the jar in the centre.

"Stand back everyone. I want the breeze to get to it," he said.

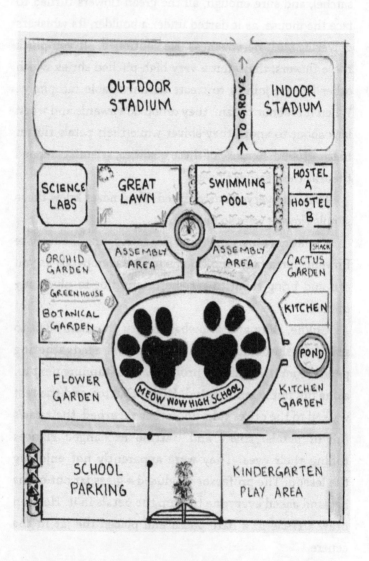

Map of the school with botanical gardens on the left

As the zephyr engulfed the petals, they rose in a slow dance and started circling around, pointing in the wind's direction. Slowly, the petals started rotating rhythmically.

"If you count the rotations per minute, you can determine the wind velocity."

Hisky and Gattino were not concentrating on the lesson. Gattino started imitating the petals and danced to an invisible beat, while Hisky made faces and giggled.

"Gattino! Hisky!" Professor Ensure called out sharply.

"Yes, sir?" Hisky and Gattino stopped giggling.

"I have been noticing your levity towards this subject since the beginning. Don't say I did not warn you. It's sticky tree detention for you both today."

The sticky tree was a large evergreen tree next to the school's greenhouse. It looked like a banyan tree but had markedly different characteristics. The hanging vines secreted a sticky sap. Its large branches created a base at the top of the trunk where few could sit. Hisky and Gattino climbed the base with the help of the gooey sticky vines that repeatedly stuck to them. Hisky and Gattino's detention was to write ten paragraphs about the Lantana flowers while seated on the branches.

"Ew," said Hisky, making himself as comfortable as he could.

"The base is sticky too," said Gattino.

They sat down reluctantly and started writing, while the class continued below them. The sticky vines splayed around in the breeze, getting into their fur from time-to-

DEFENDERS OF MEW SCAPE AND THE CORE FULCRUM

time. It wasn't a pleasant experience. Soon, they completed the session and started walking out of the garden for their snacks break. Hisky and Gattino could not get up on their own and hollered for assistance. With assistance from others, they unstuck themselves, submitted their detention work and dashed off to wash themselves, much to the amusement of the other kittens. Snowball winked at Hisky who glared back at him.

Amuse yourself as much as you can right now. My time will also come, he thought.

The cafeteria was on the ground floor of the school building next to the school pool and musical fountains. It was in a large, airy room and bustled with activity. A few posts and tables hung from the ceiling, a few of them hung from the sides of the walls, while others were on the floor. It looked like a fairy-land with beautifully engraved and painted furniture in pink, blue, white and gold. Winged waiters and waitresses fluttered around serving the kittens. The wings were not natural, but motorized ones attached to their backs. Hovering, winged trays made their way between tables, serving the snack of the day, usually cooked by Professor Piquant's class of *kitdents*. Today it was silver-batwing fritters. The open kitchen was in a large, circular, glass-walled section in the centre of the cafeteria. Everything was spick and span even when it was so busy. The chefs and their assistants cooked and hollered, placing the dishes on the flying trays and serving counters. The head chef was Mr. Samosa, and he was a large boisterous cream-coloured cat, screaming out orders to the other staff members.

Kattie, Clawcia and Melowflues climbed a vertical pole to grab a ceiling table with four chairs. Just below them sat Billy, Snowball, Goldie and Tufty at a floor-level table. On the far end, they could see Hisky, Gattino, Ruffsaw and Mewtiony settled at a side-wall table. They sat in deep discussion, their furry tails twitching and waving around. Tufty - who looked much better since his Grotider debacle, was dying of curiosity about the 'Curiosity' class.

"Hey what happened in the Curiosity class? My tests are today since I was absent yesterday. Anything you tell me will benefit me," said Tufty. He did not know about the oath.

Snowball and Goldie looked at each other and wondered how to tell him. They shook their heads at him.

"You know I also chose that as an optional subject, so you can tell me," Tufty insisted.

Snowball felt there would be no harm since Tufty would take the oath too, so he opened his mouth to tell him. No words came out and his mouth twisted itself into a complete spiral and closed shut.

Goldie was shocked, "No Snowball! We cannot talk about it!" he said.

"Ooh, woof, ah wow," Snowball said, his mouth still spiralled up like a twisted nail.

"Just stop talking! Your face will settle down." Goldie said, looking aghast.

Tufty, thoroughly scared and confused by now, looked from Snowball to Goldie. Billy, too, looked surprised. He had seen nothing like this before.

"What's wrong with you Snowball?" Billy asked.

The fluttering waitress, Gourmetty had just stopped at their table to take orders when she noticed Snowball's twisted face.

"Oh my. You look like you have eaten something special today," she said looking both amused and alarmed.

Still trying to explain himself, Snowball's eyes widened until they were twice the normal size, and his mouth elongated into the shape of a long, twisted spiral. Melowflues noticed Snowball's face from above and squealed. Clawcia and Kattie followed her glance and meowed in shock, their paws on their mouths. Their squeals and mews caught everyone's attention. Soon everyone looked at Snowball and laughed. Snowball desperately tried to open his mouth in vain. Hisky noticed Snowball from the other end and told the others at the table to look at him. They all did and burst into laughter. Mewtiony clutched his abdomen and laughed so hard, he looked like he would start rolling on the floor. Soon everyone in the cafeteria was giggling. Snowball got the message and kept quiet while his mouth slowly untwisted and became normal again.

"We cannot talk about it." Goldie told Tufty firmly. Tufty and Billy nodded in acquiescence.

Snowball felt more humiliated because Hisky had the chance to laugh at him.

Goldie, Snowball and the gang ordered Oyster sandwiches, Grasshopper milkshake and took a few bowls of batwing fritters from the hovering trays. Tufty shifted the conversation to other safer topics. Kattie, Melowflues and Clawcia ordered worm pasta, Tuna burgers and took a few bowls of fritters too. Everything was as delicious as usual. As they were finishing, Hisky and his gang walked up to Snowball.

"Can't keep an oath, eh?" Hisky winked at Snowball and walked off towards the pool with his giggling gang. Snowball glared helplessly at their disappearing backs.

The next hour was a free one, so Goldie proceeded to the library and Snowball accompanied him. Melowflues and Clawcia wanted Kattie to show them some gymnastics, so they headed off to the school gym, which was inside the indoor stadium. Billy and Tufty walked around the pool and fountains. They wanted to discuss Snowball's strange reaction, which had thoroughly jittered them both.

Following the diligent wasps which showed them the current map of school, Goldie and Snowball arrived at the massive school library on the second floor.

CHAPTER FIVE

The Pivot Evolution

The massive oak doors opened, and two books ran out, followed by two brown and furry bookends. Bookends were cats that were particularly lazy. They spent hours lying next to books to support them with their bodies. Though the pay was not high, this was one of the most coveted jobs in the world as they could catch up on many hours of sleep while working and get paid for it as a bonus. Surprised at seeing the running books, Goldie and Snowball stopped in their tracks. The books jumped over them like they were minor obstacles of a hurdle race.

"Stop! It's not your hour off today!" the bookends said as they ran after them -- in hot pursuit.

The door opened again, and the librarian peeped out. It was Mr. Pustak, one of the most senior staff members at the school. He had grey-and-pink-striped fur with a big bald patch on his head. His spectacles hung on the edge of his nose as he peered at them.

"Oh dear. Those books on travel are so difficult to control. They are always developing wanderlust. Please come in dears."

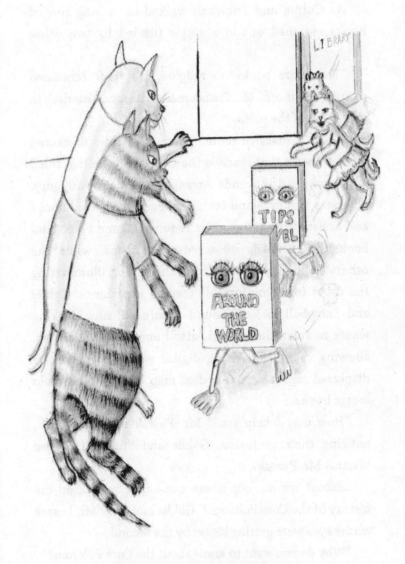

Two books run out of the library

"Thank you, sir."

As Goldie and Snowball walked in, a long row of books marched out in a single file led by two other bookends.

"Those are books on religion. It's their scheduled monthly hour off." Mr. Pustak made his way to his desk in the centre of the room.

It was a massive room. There were rows of carved wooden racks that reached the two-storey ceiling, filled with books and bookends. Arranged together by category, all books had eyes and feet. Bookends supported books and assisted the librarian as required. Some books and bookends curiously observed the kittens, while the others slept. Lights hung from the ceiling illuminating the room for a comfortable reading experience. Goldie and Snowball looked around -- confused, not knowing where to start. Sign boards also hung from the ceiling, showing categories. A big digital panel in the centre displayed an interactive index, map, and guide to help locate books.

"How may I help you?" Mr. Pustak smiled at them, noticing their confusion. Goldie and Snowball walked towards Mr. Pustak.

"Excuse me sir, but where can I find a book on the history of the Core Fulcrum?" Goldie looked at Mr. Pustak whose eyes were getting bigger by the second.

"Why do you want to know about the Core Fulcrum?"

"We also would like information about the Pivot," Snowball chimed in.

"Who told you about the Pivot? This is confidential information." Mr. Pustak looked anxious.

Snowball remembered his reaction in the café and was careful about revealing information.

"Professor Inabaox? Curiosity kills the cat? Does any of this ring a bell?" he asked allusively.

Realisation dawned on Mr. Pustak's face as he enquired, "You must tell me the name of the herb."

"Valerian." Goldie said.

The librarian looked relieved.

"Good. Just to let you know, I am also part of the club, so nothing will happen to you. Can't be too careful though, what with the Core Fulcrum stolen. Please follow me."

They walked to the rear of the room until they were in front of a locked door.

"We have to protect secrets," Mr. Pustak said, as he opened the large lock with two separate keys. The door opened into a room that was entirely blue. The room had reading tables in the front and racks behind, with blue walls, blue racks, blue books and blue bookends. Goldie felt all eyes trained on them.

"Essbound, please show these *kitdents* the book on the history of the Core Fulcrum and Pivot. I will return to my seat in case someone else needs me. However, be careful. Even walls have ears sometimes." Mr. Pustak looked at them pointedly before he shut the door behind him as he left.

Walls have ears? Who would want to snoop on us here? wondered Snowball.

Goldie and Snowball well knew that they were probably risking their lives by digging up confidential information, but now it was their duty. Essbound, a furry blue cat with blue eyes jumped off the third row of the rack on the left. She ran to the rear and called them. Goldie followed her and gasped. All the books here looked beautiful with iridescent blue covers and big blue eyes. Their eyes followed them as Essbound located the right book. She clapped her paws at it and it jumped into her arms.

"Here, you will find the information in this book and if you don't, you can check other books in the same row," having handed them the book, she went back to her place to resume her power nap.

"Be careful zzz," she said and promptly fell asleep in her rack.

Goldie and Snowball found a table with comfortable cushioned chairs to set down the book and start reading. They couldn't wait to unearth the truth. The title of the book was:

The Pivot Evolution

By Balience Walkins and Katian Agiles

The Big Catastrophe

The book started with a history of the world, and credited the evolution of cats to the unfortunate event that wiped out dinosaurs sixty-five million years ago, when a large meteor crashed into the earth. The fragments from the explosion fell back through the atmosphere, heating it so much that almost everything got burnt. If the heat did not kill the reptiles, the resulting smog blocked out the sun for many years and slowly killed all of them because of the cold. Had the resulting conditions had not wiped out dinosaurs after that catastrophe, cats as we know them today wouldn't have existed.

Miacid

The book then detailed the evolution of cats. It contained several notes about how scientists unearthed the remains of Miacids, an extinct species of mammals that lived sixty-two to thirty-four million years ago. Prehistoric archaeologists believed they were the ancestors of all carnivorous animals, including cats. Some of them lived in trees, and the others lived on the ground. They had a long tail that they waved when they were being aggressive and had long claws.

This is a Miacid

Proailurus

The book contained several articles describing these extinct mammals that lived around twenty-five million years ago. In terms of evolution, archaeologists identified them as the origin of all cats, civets, mongoose and other viverrids. They drew this conclusion after examining several fossils and bones from prehistoric ages. They noted a similar skeletal structure to ones of modern cats and viverrids.

Pseudaelurus

The book detailed the next step of evolution as the one from Proailurus to Pseudaelurus. These extinct prehistoric cats, also termed as the last common ancestor of all modern cats, lived twenty to ten million years ago. Pulosa, the god of all cats was a Pseudaelurus. They found evidence of his reign during prehistoric times in the old underground ruins at the Scratinea mountains, where scratched drawings on the cave walls, dating back to ten million years, still exist.

"It is fascinating to note that with evolution, the variety of species keeps increasing. During the beginning of evolution, there were a few species and all of them had a similar way of life. With time, each specie branches into several sub species for a specific purpose and way of life," Goldie explained aloud.

"Who knows where this might lead? Cats with wings, cats with fish scales and cats with trunks, who knows?" Snowball gave Goldie an impish smile.

"I would leave the option with the trunk out," Goldie rejoindered and continued reading.

Felidae

The current family of cats -- domestic, wild, big, and small, falls under this group. There are two main sub families known as the Pantherinae and the Felinae. The Pantherinae are the big cats and the Felinae the small cats. Felidae is the family name for all the small cats in the world. Scientists sometimes address them as felids. These cats established the first known civilization in the world. They built cities, roads, palaces and other notable structures.

Snowball paused in the middle of reading to comment aloud.

"So, we are officially the felidae or the felids! It feels cool to belong to the most civilised group in history!"

Goldie acknowledged and continued perusing.

First Civilisation

The book then traced the beginning of the first cat civilisation to thirty thousand years ago somewhere in Egytica. At the same point in time, canids started moving from forests into civilised towns and endangered felids. Canids were an animal race different from the felids. The felids were not as fast as the canids -- who started attacking their towns and homes and their numbers started depleting. The monarch King Skatzer who ruled Egytica, built large fortresses to protect the living and tombs to bury the dead in hundreds. As the numbers of the dead continued to grow, despondency took over. The remaining survivors -- a few hundred at the most, retreated into the mountain caverns to take refuge.

Canids Defeat the Felids

The canids were waiting for this moment. At the opportune moment, they conquered Egytica and destroyed its most precious structures. The king of the canids, known as King Kuthra moved into King Skatzer's palace and named it Naipada. The felids suffered a humiliating defeat. They avoided extinction by staying in the mountains and the forests surrounding them. King Kuthra's soldiers did not leave them alone even then. They kept hunting the felids during their weekly expeditions into the forests. There were 'kill or capture at sight' orders. King Skatzer, in the meantime, created a group known as the Council of Uprising of Pro felids, or the COUP, to plan the recapture of Egytica. However, the last straw was when King Kuthra's guards kidnapped King Skatzer's beautiful daughter -- Meosera, and imprisoned her in the palace. They tortured her mercilessly to get her to reveal the location of the treasury and other secrets.

"Those brutal canids!" Goldie muttered irritably. The book transported them to ancient times, and they felt every experience as though it was real. Snowball could feel his heart beating hard in his chest as he read about the atrocities Meosara and the other felids experienced as prisoners of war. The canids spared no one.

Secret experiment

King Skatzer called for an emergency meeting of the council. During that meeting, his most intelligent architect and visionary called Doctor Diadoms spoke up. He was also the chief designer of Egytica.

"Your majesty, I have been working on a secret experiment for many years. I thought I would present it before you when all the tests are complete. Most of the tests have been successful, and I needed six more months to finish the remaining ones. However, given the situation, we have no time to waste."

The monarch wanted to see what he was referring to.

Dr. Diadoms clapped his paws, and two assistants walked in with a large floating object between them. The object wasn't visible since they had covered it with a red velvet cloth, but the spectacular light patterns below it, on the floor, were, even in the dimly lit cavern. Everyone gasped in awe as they removed the cloth to reveal an iridescent cube which slowly rotated and hovered, a few inches off the ground. The light created bright patterns all around lighting up the room in dazzling colours.

"What is this thing? What is this secret experiment?" The emperor could barely sit straight on his makeshift rocky throne.

"This your majesty is what I call the Fulcrum. The Core Fulcrum."

"Why do you call it by that name?"

"The reason for that is that it can turn everything around and change the fortunes of those that possess it by giving them extraordinary powers."

The emperor's previously anxious eyes were now shining. "What powers? Show me."

The Secret Revealed

"First, one would have to consume a special juice. The juice of the Valerian herb."

The assistants brought a jar of green juice and several cups. Each of the council members drank a cup of the juice -- almost gagging on it.

"Ugh. This had better be useful. It tastes so nasty!" The emperor fell onto the floor in a puddle, like wax melting from a candle, before re-assuming his original shape. Everyone in the cavern had similar reactions. As soon as everyone went back to their normal state, Diadoms began his presentation.

"Now each one of you and your future generations will be thrice as strong and agile than ever before. With advanced flexibility, you can bend your backs to touch your nose to your rear toes and jump ten times higher. Your claws and sense of balance will be sharper than ever before. The light of the Core Fulcrum reacts with a body of a felid to make it super strong and agile."

"What about the Valerian juice?"

"That juice prevents the drinker from revealing this secret to anyone else and there is more."

"What is that?"

Extraordinary power

Dr. Diadoms asked King Skatzer to step forward and place his paw on top of the Core Fulcrum - which he did. As soon as he touched the cube, a laser like beam radiated from the cube and pierced through his paw, like a volcano, and fell like soft snowflakes around it, before disappearing in thin air.

"Now touch or aim at that large rock while thinking of the Core Fulcrum." Dr. Diadoms pointed to a rock at least a hundred times bigger than King Skatzer.

As soon as King Skatzer did that, a laser beam emanated from his paw and blasted into the rock, reducing it to vanishing snowflakes, until nothing of it remained. King Skatzer's expression said it all.

"Is there anything more the Core Fulcrum can do?"

"The Valerian power lasts only for a day. After that, you would need another cup. However, do not use this power over once a month, or it slowly diminishes. There are other powers that I will reveal the next time," Dr. Diadoms said.

"As long as the lustrous cube's light works, you and your descendants will enjoy extraordinary powers. All you need to know is how to invoke them."

"Enough said. We need to use this power immediately against the canids to rescue my daughter and recapture Egytica," said the monarch.

Felids Win Again

The rest is history. The felids, with the help of the Core Fulcrum, gained extraordinary powers that transformed them into super beings with great agility, dexterity, speed, intelligence and magical abilities. They soon defeated the canids in Egytica. King Kuthra and his followers beat a hasty retreat into the forest and those that did not leave disappeared like vapour. King Skatzer's soldiers rescued Meosora, and the king ruled Egytica once again. He rebuilt more imposing structures over the ones the canids had destroyed. The felids, with their newfound strength and agility, were almost impossible to attack and defeat now. Well, almost.

The Pivot Emerges

Zehisser, one of Dr. Diadoms's assistants got sick of living in his shadow and tried to take credit for one of his ideas. Dr. Diadoms found out and had him imprisoned. Zehisser escaped and ran away. He soon found King Kuthra -- who had made a home in the savannah grasslands close to the surrounding Thacar desert. When Zehisser told him the secret of the Core Fulcrum, King Kuthra welcomed him with open arms. He, along with King Kuthra's scientists, worked on an anti-Core-Fulcrum object. It was the darkest, most heat-and-light-absorbing, black object ever created. It could reduce or nullify the power of the Core Fulcrum by absorbing all its light. Without the power, the felids would become helpless beings and an easy target once again. King Kuthra named the object 'the Pivot' and kept it in a secret place to use it when the time was right.

The book abruptly ended on that note. There was no more information on what happened to the Pivot after they created it.

"So much for the evolution of the Pivot," Goldie said. He felt enlightened yet disappointed.

"I was hoping it would reveal *the location* of the Core Fulcrum *and the* Pivot," said Snowball, equally disappointed. "Maybe that information is in a different book," he suggested.

"Professor Inabaox mentioned that only three cats in the world know their locations, so I doubt that information would be readily available in a book. We may glean some additional clues from another book though."

Just then, they heard tiny footsteps on the wooden floor below them. Goldie's hackles rose as he peered down at the floor, expecting the worst. However, it was just a blue-eyed book standing there, eagerly proffering its arms to pick it up. The title of the book was 'Secrets of the Core Fulcrum'. Essbound was fast asleep on the rack so it meant the book had intuitively made its way to them.

Interesting serendipity, thought Goldie.

Just as the kittens excitedly bent to pick up the book, the door flew open. It was Mr. Pustak.

"Hello *kitdents*. There is someone in the library who has urgently requested the same book. Now book '1315', please run to me," he said.

"But sir, we wanted to read...," Goldie could not finish protesting, as the book jumped from Goldie's paws, to run to Mr. Pustak, blinking its eyes.

"Goldie, we must get our paws on that book. Is he even allowed to take it out of the library?" Snowball whispered.

"Snowball, let's request the borrower of the book to let us have it for a day," Goldie placed the evolution book back in the rack and started for the door just as Mr. Pustak re-entered.

"Sorry. Since he had a letter from Professor Inabaox authorizing him to borrow the book for a day, I had to hand it over urgently," he said.

"Who was the *kitdent*? I mean, what is his name?" Goldie enquired.

"He mentioned his name is Hisky."

The antagonist strikes again, thought Goldie, as Snowball and he ran out of the room, to see Hisky exiting the library, clutching his bag, with a look of great satisfaction writ all over his face. *How unfortunate!*

* * *

CHAPTER SIX

Kitdart

As the free-time slot was almost over, Goldie and Snowball exited the library too. Mr. Pustak locked the secret room as soon as they left. Their disappointment at the loss of the book was palpable.

"It feels like we lost a very important piece of the whole puzzle in the last minute. Hisky has good timing," said Goldie sarcastically.

"Hisky does not have good intentions. Even though he is part of the Curiosity Club, he is acting out of self-interest. He does not care about retrieving either the cube or the Pivot. I am sure he is doing this just for good grades and for adulation from his bootlicking fans," said Snowball.

"He will never return the book and will endanger all of us because of the delay in comprehending the truth."

"We need to devise a strategy to take the book away from him." Snowball's eyes lit up as he whispered something into Goldie's ears, and Goldie looked at him conspiratorially.

That afternoon, everyone had to attend Kitdart training lessons, which were being held in the sports' indoor stadium. As soon as Goldie and Snowball reached the venue, Tufty and Billy ran towards them.

"Purr, purr, I passed! I passed! Now I too am a Curiosity Club member." Tufty jumped around them happily; his tail swished around him and the tuft on his head bobbed merrily.

They butted their heads together in a show of friendship and acknowledgement.

"Now do you realize why I couldn't speak about it?" Snowball asked Tufty.

"Yes. I am sorry for putting you in a twisted spot."

"No worries, we have lots to tell you. Sorry Billy," said Snowball as he whispered in Tufty's ears.

They laughed together and shook paws in agreement.

Billy looked as dazed as earlier with all the secret talk, but did not dare to ask.

All the fifth-graders soon assembled in the indoor stadium that contained the training tracks for Kitdart and all the body strengthening gym equipment. The outdoor stadium had the actual Kitdart track, meant for capable and skilled *kitdents*. The main stadium also had areas for athletics and other games featured in the Catalympics. The *kitdents* used the indoor stadium only for internal training. Hisky and Gattino sat on the far end along with Mewtiony, in a deep discussion as usual. Hisky kept glancing at them from time to time, but they could not read his expression from the distance. Maybe their discussion was about the library book. Goldie wondered where he had kept it and was itching to lay his hands on it.

Soon they heard the whistle blow as Coach Dudgeble entered the stadium, rolling himself forward.

"*Kitdents--queue* up at the Kitdart training track. I would like to test your skill-level before training starts. Attach your safety harnesses."

Safety harnesses hung from sliding hooks attached to circular iron pipes that ran the length of the circular race tracks. The ceiling supported the entire safety system. There were six tracks overall, with five sections each of increasing difficulty. The sections were: Dart, Climb, Balance, Strike and Jump. Though the sections sounded simple enough, the obstacles placed around the tracks raised the difficulty level. During training, it was an individual effort, but during the Catalympics, it was a team event.

In the Dart section, there were many mobile tunnels on the track. Some of these tunnels were narrow--requiring an almost exact aim through its centre. In addition, they had the tendency to move sideways--either to the left--or the right. Intermittently, objects would drop from the pipe on the top onto the track. During the practice session, the school used objects made of paper or jelly. During the actual event, these objects could be rocks, rotten fruits and vegetables, or small animals. During Catalympics, they placed tunnels made of sand on the tracks, which could collapse at the slightest nudge from the passing *kitdent*. The objective was to be the fastest to clear the track without getting stuck in a tunnel or getting hit by an object. They would lose five points for every hit by an object and gain ten points for crossing the tunnel smoothly. Missing or collapsing a tunnel would cost ten points. Each *kitdent* would get three trials every week until the day of selection. Ten best *kitdents* got nominated on that day to represent the school for Catalympics. Catalympics was the main inter-school sporting event that every *kitdent* eagerly awaited.

Melowflues, Clawcia, Kattie, Mao, Pompom and Cica were the first to start. They wore safety harnesses and stepped in the front, waiting for the whistle to blow, while the others clapped their paws and swished their sleek tails in encouragement. There were twenty tunnels to cross, and they did not know how many objects would drop. At the blow of the whistle, they were off! Cica and Kattie took the lead as they darted across their tracks through all the shifty tunnels. Paper objects fell; one after each tunnel, and the two of them avoided most of them. Pompom's furry, pink tail got stuck in the very first tunnel as it was much bigger than her body. Melowflues got hit by almost all objects, and Clawcia missed at least four tunnels. Mao was just behind Cica when three objects hit her. Kattie and Cica led the scoreboard with a two-hundred and hundred-and-ninety-five points each at the end of the race. Cica had got hit by the last object, and Kattie had narrowly escaped. All her gymnastics training had helped her. She completed the race in fourteen seconds. Coach Dudgeble and his assistant had to dislodge Pompom from the cardboard tunnel. She looked visibly pink. Both Kattie and Cica looked sprightly as they removed the harnesses and everyone congratulated them when they walked over to the edge of the track.

The next batch of *kitdents* participated in the Dart section with similar results. Only two of the participants could complete the race. Katzchen, Misty, Hirra and Yavru missed over three tunnels each and got hit by so many objects, it was hard to keep count. Grimis was the top scorer with one-hundred-and-seventy-five points followed by Tufty with one-hundred-and-sixty points. Grimis completed the race in fifteen seconds. He sat huffing and puffing at the end of the track, glad that he had completed the race at the top. Coach Dudgeble patted him on his shoulder to encourage him. His face glowed with an inconspicuous smile.

It was time for the final group. Hisky, Mewtiony, Gattino, Snowball, Billy and Goldie fastened their safety harnesses.

"Here we go!" said Goldie when the whistle blew.

They set off like rockets, kicking dust behind them as they darted on the sandy track as fast as they could. Goldie saw the first tunnel and predicted it would shift right--looking at its movement. He was correct! As quickly as he could, he darted to the right and through it. All the *kitdents* in this batch went through the first five tunnels and dodged the supervening objects effortlessly. Hisky almost missed the sixth tunnel when it wobbled towards the right, but moved to the left instead. He was quick to notice its indecisive behaviour and go through it. Snowball continually struggled with the objects. After exiting the seventh tunnel, the rotten egg landed an inch away from his tail.

"Raise your tail Snowball!" shouted Goldie.

Snowball promptly followed the instructions for better success with the next object. The last three tunnels and objects were a lot trickier. Snowball, Billy and Gattino got hit by a tomato, rock, and painted-sponge. As a result, they missed two tunnels each. Mewtiony went completely off-track when the eighth tunnel confused him by jumping from side-to-side. He collided into its side with so much force that he somersaulted and landed outside the track on top of a large, fake tomato. This evoked loud laughter from the others. Hisky and Goldie were on track to finish the race together when Hisky whispered,

"I've got the book and I will find the Core Fulcrum. You will lose and I will win."

Goldie lost his focus for a second, and the last object -- an enormous fake earthworm fell on his nose as he watched Hisky race to the finish-line untouched. Hisky knew he had won full points, and he did a flip in the air to land on his paws. He had completed in fourteen seconds too. This meant that Kattie and Hisky had the top scores overall.

"Yippee! I did it!" he purred and cheered for himself. His whole gang of friends ran over to congratulate him.

Mewtiony lands on a large tomato

Goldie tossed off the fake worm, undid the safety harness and sportingly shook paws with Hisky. Then he walked towards his group of friends. They consoled him for losing five points. Snowball couldn't believe it.

"You were doing so well. What happened?" he asked Goldie.

Goldie shrugged.

"It was my mistake. Hisky talked about taking the book, and I got distracted. I should have ignored him."

"He cheated! He should not distract someone on the track. I will teach him a lesson."

"Leave it for now Snowball. Let us carry out our plan as discussed. That will be enough."

Coach Dudgeble summoned all the *kitdents* towards him to read out the results of the 'Dart' race for the day. After reading out all the scores and observations, he gave them tips on how to improve.

"It's all in your mind. We have exceptional eyes compared to all the living beings. We also can observe minute changes in our environment and react to it. Kitdart requires strength, agility and focus. You can improve these qualities with practise. I have seen *kitdents* starting at the bottom and becoming better than the rest. Do not lose hope with the outcome of one session. Keep trying and never give up. The indoor stadium is open in the mornings. If interested, you can work on my tips and practise," he guided.

"Sir, could you please demonstrate some of these skills?" asked Mewtiony eagerly. He did not want to repeat his mistakes.

"I certainly can," said the coach as he stood at the beginning of the track. Suddenly, he started spinning his round body so fast that it took on the appearance of a mini-tornado. He sped ahead that way, zipped through every single tunnel and dodged every object flawlessly. The tunnels sat in their own spots, not daring to move. Mewtiony felt his eyes spin around, trying to follow his actions. The coach completed the race in ten seconds. When he returned to the kittens, they clapped and cheered loudly.

"Wow, sir. It was truly inspiring to watch you," said Mewtiony.

"I wish I could spin that fast," said Clawcia.

"You were spinning faster than a top," said Goldie.

Everyone had something positive to say to the coach while he beamed in satisfaction. After that, he taught them about the rules of the remaining sections. The overall game had a track distance of five hundred meters divided into five sections of hundred meters each.

The Climb section tested a cat's climbing ability. The track comprised a series of twenty vertical ropes. These vertical ropes were of two types, either fixed or floating, and sometimes coated with different things ranging from insects, venomous snakes, to oil or powder. Floating ropes moved upwards and downwards at regular intervals. The *kitdents* had to use these ropes to climb to the top of the platform at the end of the track without falling, or touching any part of the body to the ground - at any point in the race. They scored five points each for climbing a fixed rope and ten points for a floating rope. They lost five points if their paws touched the ground anytime and ten points if they fell.

The Balance section started at the top of the platform. A plank of decreasing thickness connected the start to the finish. At the start, near the platform, other structures and ropes provided support for balancing. Towards the finish, there was no support. The planks vibrated unpredictably from time to time. The participants had to traverse from the starting platform to the destination on the ground without losing balance anytime. Sometimes, these planks would turn into slippery jelly, but the kittens had to keep going. They got a score of thirty points for completing the section without losing balance. They lost five points if they fell and had to heave themselves up again. There was a tank of green slushy slime just before the end point, below the plank. They had to stay on top of the plank until it touched the ground.

The Strike section tested the ability of the *kitdents* to strike and capture various objects flying at them. They would release twenty objects for every *kitdent*. During the actual race, the objects used were live vicious creatures. They could be vampire bats, vultures, sharp-clawed eagles, giant bees or other similar creatures. This race was not for the weak at heart. They received points for the number of strikes depending on the size of the object or creature and the potential threat. They received five points for smaller objects and ten points for larger ones. They lost five points if the objects hit or struck the *kitdents*. Some objects were scurrying mice, and if they caught them, they received twenty bonus points.

The last section of the race was the Jump section. Water covered this section of the track, and various floating objects rose from the water body to buzz around. There were alligators and electric eels in the water during the actual tournament, but here there were mere cartons and floating-discs buzzing in the air. The judges would award points based on the number of objects they jumped on to reach the finish line without falling into the water -- out of twenty objects. They scored ten points for each jump on a non-living object and twenty points for a jump on a living being. They lost five points if their paws touched water at any point in time. All the objects were constantly moving and were several feet apart, so this section needed supreme agility by the *kitdent* to score well. For this section, there were disc guards on duty atop floating discs in case they had to pull out a fallen kitten out of the water before the alligators and eels harmed them seriously.

The kittens were both curious and alarmed. This *was* a risky business!

"Why do we play this game? Isn't it perilous? Why would anyone want to risk their lives to play it?" Gattino asked expressing his apprehension after his debacle.

"We want to prepare ourselves against the worst calamities. The magical world we inhabit is in a delicate balance, and external influences could upset it. Who knows what those influences might be? In fact, our survival may be in danger even as we speak. We play this game not only to recognise and reward the most skilled and fittest young *kitdent*, but to build up an army of capable warriors. It is these warriors that have protected our entire world -- Eartavista perennially from vicious enemies that want to destroy us. Our enemies have failed until now, and we have continued rising from the ashes to achieve omnipotence indefatigably. We have to continue this great legacy," said the coach.

The kittens' hearts swelled with pride. Coach Dudgeble was one of the best athletes ever known to Eartavista, and they felt privileged to learn from him. Though it seemed like a daunting task, with training, they could soon take part alongside their seniors on the main race track. Goldie wanted to make it into the top-ten list and knew there was stiff competition from many others like him.

After his brief explanation, all the kittens took part in all the sections of the race at least once each. Gattino tried to avoid it the third time, but Coach Dudgeble wouldn't have any of it. After all the races, Kattie had the top score of six-hundred-and-thirty, followed by Grimis with a score of five-hundred-and-fifty. Hisky, Goldie and Cica got placed third, fourth, and fifth respectively. Goldie thought it would be best to practise the game a few times every week to improve his game. Ten other kittens, including Hisky, had the same thought.

* * *

CHAPTER SEVEN

A Book and a Chase

After the training session on Kitdart, all the kittens walked back to the school building. It was time for the first N-Counters's class. During that class, they would learn the intricacies of counting and numbers. The kittens just needed to know basics in this subject to help them navigate their world. No sooner had they reached the classroom, than the teacher walked in slowly behind them. Professor Manimore was a senior teacher, well past her retirement. However, the school retained her because of her expertise on the subject. She wore a white coat over her almost entirely black fur and covered her head with a white hat. As the class settled down, she stood in front to face them.

"Meow... good afternoon *kitdents*," she said politely, with a slightly quivering voice.

"Good afternoon, Ma'am," the kittens responded in unison.

"How are you all today?"

"Very well, thank you for asking, Ma'am."

"Good," she said, blinking her eyes.

That is when the kittens noticed that her eyes had a '-' symbol on her right eyelid and a white '+' one on the left eyelid. Her nose had a '*' on top of it and her mouth looked like '/' when it was closed. All the symbols where white. It looked as though counting was literally a part of her skin.

After all the introductions were over, she took a pouch out of her purse. As soon as she opened the pouch, several marbles flew out of it and started circling in front of her. She drew a pattern in the air, and the marbles followed the pattern. Then she asked the class,

"How many blue marbles are there in this bunch?"

All the kittens followed the marbles closely. They were experts at tracking moving objects. Snowball was the first to raise his paw.

"Yes, Snowball, what is the answer?"

"Its three marbles, Ma'am."

"Correct answer."

She asked for two volunteers to step forward, to which Melowflues and Misty volunteered. She handed a few marbles to both of them and extracted floating operators from another pouch. Under her guidance, the floating marbles and operators formed different combinations in front of them. She repeated the questions with all mathematical operators until they covered all the numbers from one to a million, and almost all the *kitdents* answered correctly. The moving marbles made counting and math very interesting. All the *kitdents* got engrossed in the lesson because of the innovative method used by the professor -- all except for one *kitdent* -- who started fidgeting in his seat. It was Hisky, and his mind was somewhere else. After this exercise, Melowflues and Misty returned to their seats.

Oblivious to any distracted *kitdent*, the professor then went on to other concepts by asking them a riddle.

"A cat posed this question to a friend. *'I have three kittens. The product of their ages is forty. Can you guess their ages?'* The friend thought about it for a while and shook her head. Hence, the cat provided another clue. *'The sum of their ages is equal to half my age.'* The friend thought about it again and still could not guess the answer. Then, the cat provided the final clue. *'Ok, my youngest kitten loves cheese cake.'* With that clue, the friend could answer the question. What is the answer, and how was the friend able to solve it with the last clue?"

They all thought about it for a while, scratching their heads, but no one could solve it. Hirra raised his paw and answered the riddle, but the answer was wrong.

"Think about it, look at all the numbers that lead to a product of forty - all the combinations, and you will solve it. I will reward the *kitdent* who solves the riddle, with a special, magical marble in the next class," she said, packing up to leave the classroom.

The last class of the day was for the optional subject. Billy, Melowflues and Clawcia headed to the music room for the class, followed by Gattino. Clawcia, Pompom, Mewtiony and others walked towards the art room. Snowball, Goldie, Kattie and Tufty thought of following Hisky discreetly to the next class. They wanted to find out where Hisky had hidden the book. They felt he would check on it once, before reaching Professor Inabaox's classroom, just to show off with his knowledge in front of the professor.

Hisky headed out towards the railing and jumped onto the elevator. They let him descend to the ground before following suit, keeping him in view. He turned to the left around the school building, along the kindergartner's garden. Once he reached the fountains, he turned in the opposite direction of the class and disappeared around the corner.

"See? What did I tell you? He has hidden the book somewhere and now wants to read it before the next class," said Goldie.

"Let us run behind him now, or we will lose sight of him," said Snowball.

They all ran as fast as they could till the fountains and turned to the right, in the direction where Hisky had gone. Now they could see him walking towards the swimming pool.

"Why is he going towards the pool?" Tufty asked, feeling confused.

"Not sure," said Goldie, slinking forward to follow him.

They took shelter in the trees next to the pool to see where Hisky would go next. Hisky went into the changing room

"I've got it. He has kept the book in a locker, in the changing room, near the pool. It is easy to get a locker assigned from the person on duty," Goldie ran faster until

Hisky sneakily takes the book

he was behind a tree in front of the changing rooms. The others followed him. The pool was empty as they usually held the classes in the mornings and evenings.

Hisky was out in a few minutes, carrying a bag over his shoulder. There was no chance of taking the book with it safely inside his bag. As he passed them, he did not notice the four pairs of eyes that followed his every move. They let him reach the fountains before leaving their hiding spot to walk behind him.

"He has the book in his bag. That is why he is clutching it so protectively," Goldie whispered.

"Maybe you are right, but how will we get our hands on it? If we take it, he will complain to Professor Inabaox who will surely punish us," said Kattie.

"You have a point. We will have to think of something today, because once he takes it home, we will never get it back," said Snowball, and the others agreed.

"I have an idea, but I am not entirely sure if it will work," said Tufty. "One senior I know once showed me reflective slates; thin sheets of slate that have glossy surfaces on one or both sides. We can usually find them next to seas, rivers and lakes."

"Yes, I have heard of those too. They capture images and store them, until we drop them in water, at which point they get washed and lose the captured images," said Goldie, with growing excitement.

"We can also place the slate on a blank paper or another blank slate to make a copy of the image," said Snowball, equally excited. Kattie clapped at the idea.

"Some mother-of-pearl slates can copy a whole book. I think Mawgix -- the senior, has those too. I saw them in his bag," said Tufty.

"Sounds like a solution. Tufty, do you think you could borrow a few from Mawgix and bring them to class? Please? This is our only chance. I will train you on what you miss in class today," Goldie pleaded. "I don't know him so it would look odd if I asked, but since you already have made his acquaintance, you could request the slates for an hour and return them to him."

Hisky had already reached the school building and jumped onto an elevator to take him to the third floor. Tufty thought about Goldie's request for a few seconds before agreeing. He left the others and took an elevator to the eighth floor. The others waited for Hisky to reach the top before they exited the bush and followed him discreetly.

When they reached the classroom, the class was already in session. Professor Inabaox was teaching about gleaning unobvious clues from the surroundings and solving puzzles. He looked very annoyed when he saw the late-comers.

"What is wrong today? There were so many of you arriving late for my class. First it was Hisky and now, it's all of you. The next time any *kitdent* is late for class, they will get detention. Is that clear?"

"We are very sorry, sir. We could not make it to the classroom in time, because he guided us towards a different place," said Snowball, biting his tongue. It was not a lie, but not the entire truth either. Goldie looked down and stifled a smile at the statement.

"That is strange. The directing-wasps are never wrong. Maybe you looked at the wrong classroom name and got confused. Anyway, please come in and sit down expediently. We have to make quick progress. Tomorrow, all of us will join an ongoing investigative mission to find the Core Fulcrum in the neighbouring counties. We have received information about its whereabouts. I want to teach all of you about our enemies, their territories and how to look for clues there."

Hisky, who was sitting next to Ruffsaw and Kuting, looked at them with a happy smirk. He seemed to think; *YOU DESERVE IT AND I HOPE YOU GET DETENTION.*

They entered the classroom and took seats as close to Hisky as possible. Goldie found an empty seat right behind him, and Kattie sat next to Goldie. They noticed that Hisky had placed the bag on the floor next to his seat. The only opportunity they had to take the book was to get him distracted. Goldie prayed for Tufty; Professor Inabaox would probably give him detention today.

Professor Inabaox started drawing a map on the blackboard of all the enemy hotspots in Eartavista near Mew Scape. The map contained the names of twelve counties. He classified these counties into different categories based on which clades of animals occupied them. The *kitdents* started copying the map in their books.

"We have two main enemies: the canids and the murids. Canids are at least thrice as large as us and run faster than we do. They have shorter tails compared to their bodies, which they wag from side to side when they are happy. They make loud noises when chasing us that sound like *growl, bark, or woof-woof*. Though they don't like the way we taste, they love to hunt and capture us. The Core Fulcrum gives us the boost to climb vertically and outsmart them. It also gives us a few more magical powers that I will reveal in this class. Without the Core Fulcrum, we will become an easy prey. I have marked all the counties inhabited by canids with a letter C. There are mainly two of them, which are: Wufcor and Barkeloma. The population of canids in these two counties has been stable for the last two decades. They do not have any monarch that rules them," he circled the counties on the map and started drawing a crisscross pattern to distinguish them. On the side, he drew a picture of a typical canid and detailed its body parts. He wrote the description of its habits and listed typical features of its territory.

Goldie was getting worried by the minute. *Where was Tufty? Hope he could get in touch with his senior and find the slates. The success of the plan depended on him.* Just as this thought crossed his mind, he saw a silver-grey tail bobbing up next to a desk -- in the front. Salmonair, a tenth-grader engrossed in copying the map, did not notice Tufty next to him on the floor -- slinking into the classroom. Professor Inabaox turned around to face the class just as Tufty ducked and darted to the rear of the room. He lay flat on the floor like a rug, with a knapsack on his back. Goldie could now see him, from the corner of his eye, behind Chaton -- a sixth-grader who was sitting in the last row. Professor Inabaox switched to the opposite side of the blackboard.

"Our other enemies -- murids, have historically been smaller and marginally slower than us, but not anymore. They are becoming bigger and craftier. They have sharper noses, larger ears, and longer tails. As you know, they have been our main staple diet, but lately, they have become very difficult to catch. They have a new king called Koresque, and he is a mole-rat bandicoot. Some of these bandicoots are much bigger and stronger than us. There are recent reports of abduction of felids from areas bordering the counties they inhabit. The three counties from where such reports have emerged are: Trapesky, Swampdura and Zewer." He turned around to face the board again to circle those counties and draw a pattern of horizontal lines to mark them. He wrote a large letter M above the pattern. He then similarly drew a murid, listed its body parts and detailed features of its territory. All the *kitdents* started copying the information in their books. A paper chit landed next to Goldie's feet, which he slowly picked up and opened. It was from Tufty.

I have one mother-of-pearl slate in the bag. Pick up the bag discreetly at the next available opportunity. It can copy a whole book. I also have placed a blank book in the bag to copy into. Place the blank book at the bottom, the slate on top of it, and then the library book at the very top.

Tufty slid the bag slowly behind Goldie's desk, unobserved by anyone else except his friends. Goldie nudged his bag off his desk onto the floor and picked up Tufty's bag instead of his own. The others barely noticed.

"The seven counties near Mew Scape that felids inhabit are: Mew Scape, Pausful Isle, Grand Cat Land, Lussian Peak, Furrybank, Cat Surf Town and Krusty Dunes. I hope you are all aware of them by now." He put dots all over on the counties belonging to felids to make it clearer.

Goldie opened the bag to have a look at the slate. It was very sleek with a width of about a centimetre. Both its sides glistened like a well-polished mother-of-pearl surface. The blank book was an almost replica of the library book -- although its cover was slightly lighter than the original. Only a very practiced eye could notice the difference. Snowball and Kattie noticed what Goldie was doing and wished Hisky would move out of his seat.

"Now I would like three volunteers for the next activity. One volunteer will represent canids, the second -- murids, and the third one -- felids. The class will not know who is which character. The volunteers will read out clues about the characters they represent, and the audience will have to guess," Professor created and shuffled chits as he spoke. The timing could not have been better.

Kattie was looking for this opportunity and she raised Hisky's arm -- to his surprise. Snowball also volunteered. Hisky opened and shut his mouth with nothing to say as Professor Inabaox announced,

"The three volunteers; -- please proceed to the front of the classroom. The others; -- please step forward to take part in this activity."

Hisky, Kattie and Snowball made their way to the front of the room as the others too stood up and stepped to the front. Goldie quickly grabbed Hisky's bag and opened it. Just as he had guessed, the blue-eyed book was in it. It blinked innocently at him and proffered its arms to lift it up. He took the blank book out of Tufty's bag, then placed the slate on top of it, and finally placed the library book on top of the slate -- as per Tufty's note. A sketched image of two books appeared on the side of the slate. The first book's colour was a solid black and the second one's white. Small black paw-prints ran from the first book to the second, and the second book slowly filled up with a solid black shade. Goldie kept looking in the front intermittently to make sure Hisky was busy and did not notice Goldie's shenanigans. In the meantime, Tufty stood up and nonchalantly joined the crowd in the front, winking at Goldie as he passed him. As soon as the second book became fully black, the paw-prints stopped emanating from the first book -- showing that the copying had completed. Goldie placed the newly copied book into Hisky's bag and placed the bag back near Hisky's seat. He placed the original library book in his own bag and walked towards the front to take part in the practical exercise.

Soon, all the *kitdents* completed the exercise and returned to their seats. Tufty too casually found a seat next to Snowball and sat down on the cushion. Hisky still looked confused and dazed about Kattie's action. Professor Inabaox turned to the class again and looked at Tufty with an unsure frown for a few seconds. Then, just as Tufty was getting nervous, he shook his head rapidly to clear his mind and continued.

"Canids and murids are both very dangerous animals. They can use a variety of weapons against us," he said, listing down the known weapons and their features. He also wrote some tips about countering each of those weapons.

He then introduced the concept of elongated-claw shots. After drinking Valerian juice, for up-to three hours, the club members had to only think about elongating their claws to attack an enemy, and it would happen. They could not use this move against another felid. The maximum distance possible for an attack was up-to two hundred metres. In twenty more minutes, he completed all the topics for the session.

"Good job *kitdents*! Now you can identify the counties, its inhabitants, and their attacking mechanisms without a problem. The council believes that the Core Fulcrum is in one of the five counties belonging to our enemies. Remember this tip -- the Core Fulcrum leaves clues when it traverses a path. The objects around its path of traversal will glimmer for two weeks. Watch out for that. In addition, blades of grass will look as though flattened by a road-roller. Watch out for that too. The only way they can get rid of the lingering marks is by using the venom of a poisonous arachnid, such as a scorpion which is an impossible task because they would need a large quantity. Now, make sure you are at the school grounds next to the dragonfly bus by eight a.m. We will leave shortly after that. Tomorrow, we will all join a large ongoing search party led by President

Skailimet. Soldiers and brave *kitdents* like you from all over Eartavista will take part in a massive drive to locate the Core Fulcrum."

Hisky and Goldie both patted their bags when the session was over. They were both looking forward to learning new secrets.

* * *

CHAPTER EIGHT

The Secrets of the Core Fulcrum

When the mouse bus dropped them off at the Tunnel-Garden bus-stop, the Manzar twins waved their friends goodbye and raced off home. They couldn't wait to read the book. As soon as they entered their house through the kitten-doors, they noticed their father sitting on a couch and drinking some milk. Mr. Paka Manzar--a very successful real estate manager, was home early. He was a ginger-and-white-coloured cat with a long, furry tail. They kept their bags in the storage closet and washed their paws before running into the living room.

"Hello twins! How was your day?" Mr. Manzar said when he saw his kittens.

"Hello Papa. Our day was exciting," exclaimed Snowball, running up to him to butt heads and hug him. Goldie also greeted and hugged him. He wondered whether to tell his father about the hunt, but decided against it after recollecting the NDA. Niamy brought two bowls of warm milk for them to drink, which they quickly lapped up. They discussed the day's proceedings at school, avoiding any discussion about the Core Fulcrum.

"How was your day, Papa? You always ask about our day, but rarely tell us anything about yours."

Mr. Paka laughed hard and told them about a new project he was working on.

"My company is working on building a new county for us, known as Hoverland. This county will entirely float in the air and will move around the world. This will end the need to use transportation to visit other counties. It will have all the envisaged facilities that a county needs to be self-sufficient and more. Also, it will be the coolest and greenest place in the whole of Eartavista. The construction for this ambitious project started today and will take two years to complete. President Skailimet is very supportive of this project."

"Maybe we could also move there once it's completed," said Goldie, imagining how fantastic it would be.

"I don't want to move anywhere. This house is the most exquisite one already," said Snowball.

Paka laughed again, his belly bouncing heartily.

"We shall see when we complete its construction. Accommodation on that island will be expensive to purchase. Most of the famous celebrities have already booked their villas because of which we have no vacant lots to buy now," he said.

An hour later, they ran upstairs to their room. Goldie opened his bag and took out the library book, which blinked innocently at him. He was so glad that he now had the original book -- while Hisky had the copy. Making themselves comfortable at the study table next to the window, they began reading.

This book also briefly covered the history of the felids until the invention of the Core Fulcrum by Dr. Diadoms. It covered a short paragraph about the invention of the Pivot too. As Goldie turned the page to read the next section, all he saw was a poem followed by a large silver paw-print on the opposite page. All the remaining pages were blank.

I am sure I brought the right book, he thought, feeling frustrated. Snowball too flipped through all the pages of the book and found nothing.

"I took the library book out of Hisky's bag and put the copied one into it. I am sure this is the original book," Goldie said, bewildered at this development.

"Let's read the poem. Maybe it will reveal a clue," Snowball suggested.

Goldie agreed and started reading the poem which read:

Here within this manuscript old
Lie magical secrets rarely told
The enlightened one may unblock
Press the right key to the lock
Tread the magical world with care
Wise one, proceed if you dare

"First, I cannot comprehend this poem. Second, it sounds like a scary challenge," started Snowball. "What key is it referring to and what lock? What does the book mean by 'proceed if you dare'?" He imagined frightening creatures appearing around them because of interacting with the book.

Goldie looked preoccupied as he tried to decipher the cryptic poem. The first two lines only seemed to imply that the manuscript was from ancient times with rare secrets written within it. He could not glean any other meaning from them. The next two lines were more cryptic and seemed to provide a hint for unlocking something: *enlightened one, press the right key to the lock*. Maybe the clue was about revealing the text in the blank pages. Enlightened ones would be those who had more clarity than others, who knew the truth as it is. *Also, usually we insert keys, not press them*, he thought. This book was looking for someone who knew the truth and had a key of the right type they could press onto a lock. What if enlightened meant members of the 'Curiosity' Club? That would solve the third line. *Press the right key to the lock*. This sentence kept repeating in Goldie's mind, while the image of the paw-print in the book kept getting bigger. It had a metallic tinge and appeared slightly raised above the level of the page.

Strange paw-print, thought Goldie. On a sudden whim, he pressed his right paw--which was of the exact size of the paw-print, on to its metallic surface. The very next second--he wished he hadn't. The paw-print descended into the book with a 'click' while Snowball watched in amazement. Why hadn't he thought of it? Wisps of rainbow-coloured lights started emanating from under the paw-print until they surrounded both of them. The two looked around themselves in awe and consternation. Suddenly, their feet lifted off the ground, and the lights started whirling around them until they engulfed them in a spinning realm of rainbow-coloured lights. The lights whirled faster and faster until they completely merged to become a spherical bubble. From the roof of the bubble descended an old smiling face belonging to a cat with long white whiskers and a white beard. There was a long silver tuft on top of its forehead. It smiled at them from the top.

"Help!" shouted Goldie and Snowball, startled at seeing the strange face staring at them. They tried to claw their way out of the spinning bubble -- in vain. The bubble bobbed up and down gently at their agitated attempts to escape its interior. They spun around and landed on their backs onto the soft surface, but stayed inside. The old cat started laughing at them, his beard bouncing up and down with the effort -- immensely amused at the spectacle.

"Hello, who are you?" asked Goldie -- panting -- as he stopped running. His body floated until he got suspended in the centre of the orb.

"I am Doctor Diadoms, a lead scientist from an ancient land," said the kind old cat.

"Are you the original Dr. Diadoms? *The* Dr. Diadoms who worked in the court of King Skatzer?" asked Snowball in bewilderment.

"That very one," answered the face.

"What do you want from us?" asked Snowball.

"I should ask you the same question, since you were reading my book," said Dr. Diadoms.

Diadoms appears through the orb

"We were reading it because we wanted to know the secrets of the Core Fulcrum. Someone stole it recently, and we hope we may glean a few clues about its current location. Once we find it, we hope to interact with it appropriately by learning about its properties. The purpose is to defeat our enemies," Goldie explained.

"I am the creator of the Core Fulcrum and know all its secrets, well almost. I do not know who stole it or where they hid it, but I can give you information about its powers and properties. Only enlightened and trustworthy felids can access me through the book. Since you accessed me, I know I can trust you," said Dr. Diadoms.

"Thank you for placing your trust in us. We will not let you down," said Snowball.

"Good, shall we begin with an introduction? While I narrate my tale, you will see the corresponding images on the wall of this rainbow orb. Pay attention to both the audio and video renditions of my story. My work on the Core Fulcrum goes back to many years before the canids attacked Egytica." As he spoke, the orb became larger until it was almost the size of the Manzar twins' room. Its surface became opaque to display moving images from Dr. Diadoms' memory. Comfortable baskets appeared on the opposite side. Goldie and Snowball promptly took the cue and sat in them.

"We, felids were a weak race and lived off the rations provided by the two-legged hairless beings. We knew we would not survive much longer, as the reports of the ferocious canids and their conquests had reached us.

Hence, my team of assistants and I started working on a project to increase our strength. We stumbled upon a peculiar mine of gems near Egytica and found an enormous ore. On extracting it, we found a rare element. It was rare because it shone brighter than a diamond and refracted light in a very unusual way. We deduced it was an interstellar object because we had seen nothing like it before in the world. An interesting property of the gem was its ability to hover over the ground. It was lighter than a feather and had electromagnetic properties. The most extraordinary aspect of the gem was that it provided unparallel strength and agility to anyone who even looked at it. Later in our experiments, we found that this power only worked on felids. Not only did it affect the current generation but changed the genetic makeup of future generations -- such was its unusual power. Since we felt its discovery was a turning point in our evolution, we called it the Core Fulcrum or the object around which our lives would revolve."

"Yes, we read about this amazing fact in another book," said Goldie.

The moving images showed a much younger Dr. Diadoms walking through dunes in a dry desert with three other assistants. All of them wore blue, hooded cloaks. An enclosed brown sack floated between the two assistants who walked in the front and two who walked in the rear. Soon they arrived at a rocky mountain. They climbed the mountain and stopped when they reached its peak. The peak contained a caldera, or a crater, at the top of the mountain. The caldera contained a self-sufficient island in the centre. The four felids took a raft with the bobbing gem to the island on the raft. There was only one cave on the island besides all the greenery. That cave was their workshop. Hidden away from the rest of the world, they were safe to work on their experiment.

"We conducted several experiments and discovered a few of its powers, but we believed there were many more. The powers we discovered were: an ability to strengthen felids and make them super agile, the power of nine lives, super sharp night vision and the ability to see through objects, the power to make objects float or hover, an ability to turn inanimate objects to live beings and vice versa, the ability to communicate with all objects in Eartavista, Valerian Laser Power to destroy anything and turn it into disappearing dust, and a special individual power unique to every felid."

Goldie and Snowball found the live narration and imagery intriguing.

"Could you explain what each of these powers are and how we can enable them?" asked Snowball. He couldn't wait to start his experiment with these powers.

"The first three powers belong to the basic group. They deal with the physical ability of felids. Agility gives them the power to jump over long distances that hitherto seemed impossible. Flexibility allows them to contort themselves and squeeze into the tiniest of spaces. With increased strength, they can lift any object at least a hundred times their own weight. The power of nine lives is self-explanatory. There is only one way to kill a felid in one shot, and that is using the Valerian Laser Power, which, incidentally only a few distinguished felids can do. All other falls and accidents only take one life. Super night vision is also self-explanatory. Basic powers of agility, strength, nine lives and night vision get inherited at birth. These powers get exaggerated when the light of the Core Fulcrum falls directly on them."

"What about the other powers like the power to make objects float, the ability to turn inanimate objects to live beings, to communicate with inanimate beings, and the special individual power? How do we enable those?" asked Goldie.

"That is why I devised this training program. It is hard for me to explain all the steps in one session. This is a four-week-long course called 'Secrets of the Core Fulcrum'. Privileged felids like yourselves have full access to it, but to unleash all the powers, you need to attend two sessions every week. I will teach you everything about every power one-by-one. If you have the skill, the sky is the limit. Once you complete this training, you can move onto more advanced topics and train to become a Goldermew. A Goldermew level is the highest distinction in the cat-world, which they now call Eartavista," said the wise one.

"Four weeks is too long. We have to complete this course as soon as possible. If our enemies understand how to use its powers, they will destroy us. A large group, including us, will depart on a drive to search for it tomorrow and hope to locate it. Once we locate it, we can enable its powers and use them to stop the enemy," Goldie pleaded.

"The reason this course is unhurried is that we don't want it to fall into the wrong hands. Sometimes evil felids use these powers for the wrong purpose, and instead of becoming a Goldermew, the felid becomes a Fiendyowler, a dangerous being bent on destruction. The only felid that can attack another felid is a Fiendyowler. Pray that you never see one," said Dr. Diadoms.

Fiendyowler? Sounds dangerous, thought Snowball.

"We need your help urgently, Dr. Diadoms. Without your help, it may be impracticable to complete the course. We really do not have that much time. How do we convince you we will never become Fiendyowlers?" said Snowball.

"I need two more enlightened felids to join you for the course. Can you find them? If they join, I will cast the square bond spell on all of you, and none of you will ever become a Fiendyowler. In that case, I can complete the course in four days, one session per day."

"What do you mean by enlightened felids? The book uses that term, and you too mentioned the phrase earlier." Snowball looked curiously at Dr. Diadoms' face.

"Enlightened felids are those who have drunk Valerian juice given to them by a Goldermew. Goldermews have the special ability to pass down enlightenment to other felids through the magical Valerian plant. Fiendyowlers lack this one ability and that is why they despise us."

Now it all made sense to Goldie and Snowball. The reason they could activate the training program through the book was because they had drunk Valerian juice during the first session of the 'Curiosity' class, becoming enlightened. That also meant that Professor Inabaox was a Goldermew. Not only were they both enlightened, so were all the others from the 'Curiosity' class. That explained why cats ate grass sometimes, including Valerian stems. They had magical and healing powers.

"Valerian grows everywhere. Isn't it dangerous to attach such super powers to something that is abundantly available?" asked Goldie.

"Yes, wild Valerian grows everywhere, but only the juice given to you by a Goldermew goes through a special process, providing it with magical properties. To access the express training program, you would have to bring two more enlightened felids into the orb. Would you be able to do that?"

"Yes, we have two more friends, who can be part of the square bond. If you help me exit this orb, I will call them the next time," said Goldie.

"That is easy. Just say the words 'exit rainbow rondure' or 'exit rondure', and you will be free. To re-enter the orb, you will need to press the paw in the book again."

They both said 'exit rainbow rondure' simultaneously. First the baskets disappeared, followed by the face, and then the orb stopped spinning until only wisps were visible. The wisps disappeared into the book, and the two kittens dropped slowly onto the floor.

"What should we do? Should we call Kattie and Tufty home now, or wait until we have some clues about the

Core Fulcrum's whereabouts?" whispered Goldie to Snowball.

"It's late now--not sure if they can leave their homes after dark without seeking prior permission. Why don't we talk to them both after the outing tomorrow? That way, we can bring them up to speed about the book after the trip and perform the orb exercise together. We could find a quiet, undisturbed place for this exercise. I am afraid that Mom and Dad will discover what we are up-to if we continue invoking the orb at home," Snowball told his brother.

"You are right. This has been an important discovery for us and a big leap forward in the investigation about the Core Fulcrum. We should continue tomorrow," said Goldie and kept the book back in his bag. They both proceeded downstairs for dinner. Niamy had made hot prawn pie and earthworm noodles for dinner. As a welcome gesture, she gave them both back rubs, and they purred in response.

In the northern-most suburb of Mew Scape, called Slippery Dews, Hisky struggled with the book. He tried everything he could, but the book's pages stayed blank after the first ten pages. Invisible ink readers also did not help much. Frustrated, he threw the book on the marble floor, and it started crying. Big drops of blue tears leaked from its eyes onto the floor until there was a large, messy puddle in the room.

* * *

CHAPTER NINE

Airborne in a Dragonfly

The next morning, all the 'Curiosity' club members assembled near the dragonfly bus. Its wings were already whirring to start the warm-up process. A spherical cluster of blue-green, shiny beetles that emitted rays of light in the dark formed its eyes. The pilot of the bus sat in a cabin hanging from its jaws. The two attendants each sat in a small bubble on top of its antenna. Professor Inabaox stood by it with his two assistants Pusa and Yata. He shouted over the whirr of the wings,

"Everyone, please note that once you enter the bus and take your seats, the assistants will hand over vials of Valerian juice, binoculars and CLG shots to everyone. CLG stands for compressed lemon grass. These tools will help you look for clues and keep you safe. When we board, we will guide you on how to use these tools. Now follow me in," he said, climbing the bus using a scratching post on its side.

Soon they were all seated. Goldie, Snowball, Kattie and Tufty sat in its thorax while Hisky, Ruffsaw and Kuting made their way to the long, segmented, abdomen section. There were eight seats in the thorax and nine seats in the long abdomen. Hisky looked particularly upset and gestured to Ruffsaw about something. Salmonair, Chaton, Seabreeze, Pilli, and two other club members followed them and sat down in the rear. Goldie and Snowball knowingly glanced at each other and thought of talking about their experience with the book when there was more privacy. It was not safe to talk about it when so many others surrounded them. The pilot allotted the front row of seats to Professor Inabaox and his two assistants. The assistants walked around, distributing the vials, binoculars and CLG shots, which looked like paw sized cat-claws, with a hole in the narrower side and a triggering button on the broader side. After everyone had received the tools, Professor Inabaox and his assistants walked to the middle of the bus to start the guidance. His voice was loud enough to reach the rear.

"Listen carefully everyone. As we fly over enemy territory, I will call out the name of each county. I would like each of you to look for clues as I explained in the class yesterday. I also provided tips on how to recognise our enemies, their territories, and how to tackle them in case you directly encounter them. This is important--to target correctly. We should not harm any innocent beings. Besides the elongated-claw attack mechanism, please use these CLG shots for your defence and to take down the enemy. When you press the trigger behind the CLG shot, a claw will shoot out to cover a distance of up-to five hundred metres. The shot will only tranquillize the target. We cannot use this weapon against another felid. That is all I wanted to tell you -- questions?"

Many paws went up one by one to ask questions, and Professor Inabaox answered all of them patiently. Once he had satisfactorily answered them, Professor Inabaox spoke more encouraging words to give them courage. Everyone looked slightly nervous yet excited to begin the adventure.

"I wish us all the very best of luck. I am positive we will be successful today." He made a thumb-up sign and walked to his seat in the front. His assistants followed him, and they all sat down.

As the dragonfly started slowly walking on the long runway strip next to the parking zone, the attendants stepped forward. They were two skinny cats dressed in metallic red dresses with beautiful red bows around their heads. One of them removed a yellow hibiscus from a vase and held it in front of her mouth. It turned into a brass loud speaker. The other attendant walked in the front facing all the passengers. She held a snake, a jellyfish, a large folded sponge with seaweeds all around it and a card in her arms. The one holding the loudspeaker started talking. While she talked, the other one demonstrated safety procedures using the objects and beings she carried.

"Please listen to these safety instructions to enjoy a safe flight. To fasten your snakes... um... seat belts, insert the tail of the snake into its mouth. It will turn into a fastened seat-belt. It will automatically adjust itself to the size of your waist. To unfasten pull up the clasp and remove the buckle. It will turn back into a snake," she said. Looking at the alarmed looks on everyone's faces, she added, "Don't worry they are tame and will neither move nor bite. In case of an emergency, jellyfish will drop from the top panel. The jellyfish will turn into real masks as soon as you touch them. Please wear the mask with the band around your head in this manner and start breathing. Please wear your mask first before assisting others. In case of an emergency landing, you can use the life-saving kits placed under your seats. The kits contain an inflatable mushroom and a seaweed-lined sponge. They will turn into a parachute and life-jacket respectively when used. Place the sponge over yourself in this manner and fasten the seaweed around your waist. Tug the seaweed sharply to inflate the sponge and make it waterproof. Blow into the openings provided on the shoulders and manually inflate it. Read the card completely to understand more about what to do in an emergency. Thank you all."

After the attendants had completed the safety procedure, they climbed the ladders that reached the top of the antennae to take their places. The seat-belt signs were on, hence, all of them put their seat belts onthat tightened around them to prevent wobbling around during the flight. The dragonfly bus's wings started whirring faster, and as it took off, it turned into a real dragonfly. There were shouts of delight as it soared above the school and whizzed above tall treetops. Nesting painted storks gawked at them as they passed by. The little fledglings waved at the *kitdents*, and they waved happily back. This would be a very dangerous, adventurous, and highly entertaining ride.

Meanwhile, at the royal dungeon, in King Koresque's kingdom, the two hefty guards were feeling very annoyed and exhausted. The Core Fulcrum had been playing a cat-and-mouse game with them ever since they had enclosed it in a cage on the first day of its capture. After enclosing it, they wanted to lock it in one of the prison cells by the cliff. It willingly hovered along with them in the floating cage until they reached the circular garden surrounded by the cells. The garden was like an indoor atrium, covered with a bulging, bubble-glass roof. A grid of thick ropes supported the thousands of intricate glass-like bubbles on the top. They opened one prison cell and tried to guide the cube inside, but it refused to enter. They tried with many other cells, in vain. It had a mind of its own. Try as they might, they could not convince it to enter. Believing the cage was obstructing it, they thought of taking it out. The first guard named Vermish held a wooden spear, and the other one named Chooha opened the cage. Vermish poked and nudged the refractive cube out of the cage. That was his biggest mistake. The Core Fulcrum rushed out of the cage and started revolving around the circular garden continuously--just out of the guards' reach. Every time it completed a circuit, three different-coloured light rays emanated from its top to shoot up into the sky. It was like an SOS signal. Because of the bubbles on the roof, the light rays scattered into thousands of refractions and burst into the sky like noiseless fireworks.

"Chooha--catch it or we are dead meat. King Koresque will not spare us if he finds out that it's out of its cage. If someone sees those signals, they may come after it," said Vermish.

"I cannot catch it on my own. Please help me," said Chooha as he ran after it. Vermish joined him in the chase.

They ran after it for a long time--huffing and puffing--until minutes turned into hours, and hours turned into days. It stayed out of reach and continued revolving around the garden. They took turns to run after it, but ensured that one of them kept the effort up. They also tried climbing trees in the garden and ambushing it--to no avail. They tried approaching it from opposite sides, but that worked neither, since it darted diagonally to the other side and continued revolving. This was the third day of their effort to catch it. They were both dazed and exhausted. Vermish could not take it anymore.

"I... I give up. I am so... so exhausted, I can bare... barely stand," he said, wobbling towards an old Peepal tree in the centre of the atrium to lay down below it.

Chooha felt exhausted too. He stopped chasing the cube to lie down next to Vermish.

"We should inform the others. How long are we going to try catching the cube on our own?" he said.

"I am afraid of the consequences. The others will definitely inform the king. We are lucky that no one else monitors these prison cells. The secret is still with us. As I mentioned earlier, if the king finds out, it's surely the gallows for us," said Vermish.

They lay together under the tree for a long time discussing their options. They rested for so long that they did not notice the cube slowing down and coming to a standstill next to them, as though eavesdropping on their conversation.

As though by instinct, Vermish looked behind, noticed the cube and shouted,

"CHOOHA, CATCH THAT CUBE!"

Chooha jumped up as soon as he heard Vermish and lunged at the cube. Vermish sprang up too and joined Chooha once more in the chase. The cube sprang forward just as they both catapulted towards it. They missed the cube and landed ungracefully. Vermish fell face-flat into a pond infested with crabs, while Chooha landed in a pit of quicksand. Prisoners in the occupied cells pointed at them and laughed till their stomachs ached. Vermish could not open his eyes as mud and crabs covered his face. The crabs painfully pinched him everywhere.

"OW! OWW WOW OUCH!" he screamed in pain, as he desperately tried to remove the crabs. The crabs held on for dear life. They were not about to let go of their assailant easily. As Vermish pulled the leg of one crab who had caught hold of his eyebrow, another orange-coloured crab grabbed his nose and pinched it hard in response. "OW, OWW, OWW," he responded.

Chooha started sinking slowly. First his feet, then his ankles, followed by his knees disappeared into the sand.

"HEEEELP! I AM SINKING!" he called out.

"SOMEONE PLEASE HELP US!" they screamed, unable to help themselves.

The cube revolved faster around the garden, bouncing blithely as though enjoying their plight.

At that very moment, the dragonfly buzzed around until it arrived above a large swamp. A garden and a forest surrounded the muddy expanse. Professor Inabaox asked the pilot to lower the craft while he peered through the window, using his binoculars. All the other *kitdents* followed suit. They peered through the windows to look for any signs of the Core Fulcrum. The dragonfly circled around the swamp several times. Finally, it hovered close to its surface, and came to rest on a large blade of grass that offered a good view all around. All objects were larger than life in Swampdura. A variety of plants grew abundantly around the marsh with enormous leaves, flowers and fruits. Even the fallen seeds looked larger than coconuts. A few dandelions drifted in the breeze at a distance. They looked like enormous parachutes. Tufty imagined what it would be like to ride one. Giant bees and butterflies flew from flower to flower, making loud flapping sounds as they passed the dragonfly. When they drank nectar from flowers, they made audible slurping sounds. There was an enormous hibiscus plant next to the dragonfly with gigantic red flowers. As a saffron-yellow butterfly finished drinking nectar from the flower, it flew by, and a drop fell on the bus. It splashed on the *kitdents* like a whole bucket of water. Many of them squealed in response as they got thoroughly drenched. The two attendants rushed down to hand them some cotton towels to wipe themselves.

If all the animals in this county are so huge, imagine how huge the murids are, thought Snowball. *I hope we can deal with such big enemies. I don't want to die so soon.* Almost all the other passengers had similar thoughts.

While they waited with rising apprehension, an earthworm bus from Great Skats School dived into the swamp, carrying with it, screaming *kitdents*. Luckily, these underwater buses were water-tight. Maybe they had noticed something, and would find the murids underneath. It created a small splash as it dived and frightened toads jumped off lotus leaves to the rocks on the edge. The toads scolded the earthworm bus for disturbing them.

"RRIBBIT, RRRIBBIT, RRRRIBBIT!" they said, their throats bloating to the size of hot air balloons. Everyone had to close their ears to shut out the thundering sound. Eventually the toads stopped and jumped on new leaves to settle down in peace. They waited for over fifteen minutes, but the bus did not emerge. Goldie and Snowball used their binoculars, keenly scanning the landscape, as did the others. They did not find any sign of either the divine Fulcrum or a murid.

"Maybe they are all in their burrows, or they are hiding from us. I don't see any signs of the Core Fulcrum here. If there is anything interesting underneath the swamp, the earthworm bus will find it. Let us proceed to the next county," said Professor Inabaox.

If there is something interesting, I want to find it, thought Goldie.

The dragonfly lands in Swampdura

The dragonfly took off with a buzzing of its wings, and they were airborne again. In the sky, they passed by the butterfly, seagull and woodpecker buses. Those belonged to search parties from other schools. As they passed, all the *kitdents* waved at each other. President Skailimet was in the eagle bus along with a few soldiers. He nodded at Professor Inabaox in acknowledgement. They reached Swampdura as the dragonfly left.

The next flight was along a county abutting a large grassland. Large, multi-storey kennels made of sandstone dotted the landscape. Smoothly paved pathways weaved through this neat township. They could see a marketplace where town dwellers were shopping for their daily needs. A few rocky and dry hillocks flanked the town to the south and all around, with dense clumps of tall bushes surrounding them. This was the county of Wufcor. They saw a pack of approximately twenty canids skate-boarding towards the river that meandered through the vicinity. A white-coloured yacht waited at the docks. The canids had brown fur with black-coloured snouts and thick, bushy tails. The group comprised many adult canids and a few cute puppies. The puppies bounced along on the side of the adults with their tongues hanging out -- wagging their tails with glee. Maybe they were going on a family picnic. When they saw the large bus hovering above, they stopped and barked at it uneasily for some time -- backing up. The pilot lowered the dragonfly to get a better view of them and the surroundings. Feeling threatened, the largest canid -- who appeared to be the leader of the pack lunged at it. It narrowly missed grabbing Kattie's arm with its teeth. Hearing Kattie's scream, the pilot moved higher and out of reach. Except for this close shave, they encountered nothing unusual in this county either.

"Be on high alert! The next county is potentially dangerous because that is where the abductions of felids took place recently. Drink a sip of Valerian juice to activate the elongated-claw form of attack. We may need to change buses there to board one that is more appropriate to explore the territory," said Professor Inabaox, as they headed towards Zewer.

As they approached, the landscape dramatically changed to a foggy and dingy one. There were criss-crossing creeks visible in the dark, marshy terrain. Though the murids had covered many of these creeks with stone paving blocks, they had left many others uncovered, creating accident-prone zones. Bridges connected cobbled streets between the creeks. There were many lighted openings along those streets, with chimneys spewing out smoke next to them. These were the underground burrows of murids that inhabited Zewer. They scurried in and out of the lit openings with an urgent, nervous demeanour. They wore black bandanas on their heads and flippers on all their feet. In every other way, they were like typical rats that lived in sewers. A few of them carried black bags. Flat raft-like vehicles transported them around their filthy streets. A little farther, a cloud of white spores gushed upwards from a large ditch. It was a ditch filled with garbage.

As the bus hovered lower, Goldie peered through his binoculars to scan the vicinity and observe its minute details. An intrusion of Brobdingnagian cockroaches reined together in rows formed the base of the raft. The driver sat in the front on what looked like a stool made of a vacant, brown-coloured egg-sac and controlled the ten vanward cockroaches. The remaining cockroaches, in the nine rows behind them, blindly followed the leaders in the front. All the passengers sat on a bench placed on the backs of the cockroaches, behind the driver, appearing to be deep in conversation with each other. The stench in this town was almost unbearable.

YUCK, thought Goldie. I am so glad I am not a murid living here.

Hisky almost gagged when he smelled the air, but controlled himself when he saw Professor Inabaox looking at him. He did not want the professor to expel him from this prestigious club for showing signs of frailty.

As they parked on a desolated road on the outskirts of the town, they saw a bespectacled, apron-wearing, old rat, hobbling along the path. She carried a purse on her left shoulder. Suddenly, a group of bandana-headed rats emerged from the corner and accosted her. Goldie saw one rat extracting a dagger from his bag to stab her.

"HEY STOP!" shouted Goldie from the bus as the burglar grabbed her arm, ignoring her feeble protests.

Forthwith, Goldie pressed the trigger of the CLG-shot. The shot hit the dagger-carrying rat on his back. He squeaked in pain when the dart pierced him from behind.

"ITCHYKITCHYSCREEE!" he screamed the next moment, frozen to the spot. Then, with his arm still raised up--holding the dagger, he slumped to the ground. The tiny dagger fell to the side with a clink, and his companions beat a hasty retreat. By the time the *kitdents* arrived near the granny rat, the robbers had vanished. Goldie picked up her purse and handed it to her.

"Squeak! Th... Thank you dear!" she said gratefully to Goldie, taking the purse. There were tears glistening in her tired eyes. "You are a kind felid. The purse contained my only savings. I don't know how to repay you. An old granny like me has nothing much to offer."

"You don't have to repay me. I did what anyone would in the situation," he said.

"If you ever need my help, do not hesitate. I live in the burrow numbered one-hundred-and-two, at the end of this street," she said. After Goldie agreed, she thanked him profusely and continued shuffling to her burrow.

"What a waste of a CLG-shot and what a mawkish scene you created for nothing!" exclaimed Hisky. "You could have attacked him with an extended claw. Now you have one less dart left for the actual enemy," he sneered--secretly jealous that Goldie had successfully handled the errant rat. Kuting and Ruffsaw patted Hisky on his shoulder.

"If you thought it was such a great idea, why did you not do it?" asked Snowball, challenging Hisky. Kattie and Tufty nodded in agreement.

Professor Inabaox sensed the tension and walked to Goldie to pat him on his back.

"Good job Goldie. I appreciate what you did. It takes time to master all the tools and weapons. You will learn more with experience. Here, wipe your paws with sanitizer to be safe," he said, dropping some liquid on Goldie's paws, who rubbed them together vigorously. Then he said, "Let's go everyone. There is no time to waste. We need to board new vehicles that are waiting for us at the end of this street next to the bank of the largest creek."

"What do we do with this sedated rat?" asked Ruffsaw, pointing to the still murid on the street.

"Why don't we take it with us? It will make a good meal. Everyone loves to eat fresh mouse steak," said Kuting, licking his upper lip.

"We do nothing. We don't have the permission to hunt in Zewer - besides, it is not a mouse. He will rise after an hour and will not have any memory of this experience," Professor Inabaox said, looking sternly at Kuting. They were not here to hunt for their next meal. The audacity of some kittens shocked the professor.

CHAPTER TEN

Distress Call

Felidae
Aurum

They bounded together towards the bank of the creek where their next vehicles were waiting. There stood at least a dozen dome-covered gerridae or water-skeeters at the bank. *Kitdents* from several schools stood beside them, waiting in anticipation. Each vehicle could seat up to four *kitdents* along with the captain. Professor Inabaox got into the first one and signalled for everyone to enter the remaining ones. Goldie, Snowball, Kattie and Tufty got into the second one, followed by Ruffsaw, Hisky, Kuting and Salmonair, in the third one. Once everyone took their places, they were off. The water-skeeters threw a grey-coloured, slushy jet stream behind them as they 'skated' at high speed on the creek's surface. The filtering lenses attached to its feet streamed live images to the screen inside the protected dome above.

They meandered this way -- on the creek, for almost twenty minutes, until they reached a large bridge. Short buildings with pigeon-hole-like structures surrounded the bridge. This looked like the main centre of Zewer. As the captains steered the skeeters under the bridge, suddenly, a barrage of stones started hitting them. Some of these stones were very large, and the domes started cracking with the impact--which was an ominous sign. If the noxious air entered the dome, they would collapse with the unbearable stench. They saw a long row of bandana-headed rats operating catapults to launch the stones at them from the top of the bridge and from both sides of the creek.

"Don't retaliate! Just move on!" screamed Professor Inabaox from his seat.

They sped on as the distance between them and the attacking rats grew. The catapulted stones stopped reaching them. They could hear them splashing into the creek behind them. All the domes got covered with cracks and blobs of dirty water, but stayed intact fortunately. Luckily, all of them escaped unscathed. They explored all the creeks but found nothing relevant--except for a few hidden vaults, where the rats had stored stolen goods. They soon exited at the docks closest to the dragonfly bus. Secretly, Goldie and Snowball had enjoyed the adventurous water ride; stench or no stench.

Soon they were flying towards their next destination--Barkeloma. It turned out to be the most peaceful county, built around a thick jungle, with grey pyramid-like structures everywhere. Black-and-white spotted canids wearing grey robes sat levitating and meditating in these structures--undisturbed by the search operation. Bells rang in the distance to aid with their meditative chanting. They did not open their eyes even when the dragonfly whirred along the pyramids for some time.

"BROM, HROM, KROM, SHROM," they continued chanting peacefully -- their eyes closed. Hisky, Ruffsaw and Kuting looked very amused at the spectacle beneath them. The *kitdents* left this place rather quickly after surveying it for any signs of the Core Fulcrum. There were none.

They were now down to the last county -- Trapesky. Goldie felt like they would find the Core Fulcrum there. He felt it in his gut.

It was almost noon as the Dragonfly flew farther west from Barkeloma until it reached the sea-shore. Here, miles of stark cliffs lined the shore; several of which had marble streaks and glinted like mirrors in the sunlight. Their eyes squinted against the bright reflections. The county of Trapesky lay in and around these marble-faced cliffs. Behind the cliffs rose an imposing palace made completely of marble and calcite extracted from bones. Dazzling, precious gems -- collected from mines nearby, lavishly adorned the ornate structure. It was one of the most resplendent palaces in Eartavista and glistened in the light. Small houses made of marble surrounded the palace at a distance on all sides. All the *kitdents* stayed glued to their binoculars as they observed the scene below them in awe.

They should have named this county Marble-land instead of Trapesky, thought Goldie.

"Don't get taken in by the pristine nature of this county. Dangerous mole-rat bandicoots live here. King Koresque, who lives in the palace, is the monarch of all murids and has a formidable army of soldiers. Many of them are larger than us. They also boast of some of the best weapons in Eartavista. Keep your claws and CLG shots ready," said Professor Inabaox.

The dragonfly swooped down towards the marble cliffs so they could observe the terrain better. Snowball exclaimed when he saw the beautiful reflections in the marble faces.

"Wow! I can see the reflection of the dragonfly!"

They fixed their eyes onto their binoculars for the umpteenth time to magnify objects below and inspect them. An open lawn surrounded the palace, but the grass here did not look flattened. As the bus passed the palace towards the ruins further north, the well-manicured garden turned into a dense forest. because of its density, they could not see the grass below. Also, Because of the reflections from all the surfaces, it was tough to see any other clues that would highlight the radiant cube's presence.

"We will have to land and scan the forest," said Professor Inabaox, giving instructions to the pilot. "Everyone, stay on your guard. You will need to use your best reflexes."

The bus spotted a clearing after the forest and landed there as silently as possible. All of them spilled out of the bus, holding their claw-shots close to them and spread out. Goldie and Tufty walked towards the left of the clearing, while Snowball and Kattie walked to the right. Hisky, Ruffsaw, Kuting and Salmonair continued straight behind the professor. The remaining kittens spread out behind them, keeping close at hand. Their tails silently trailed behind them without touching the ground. They kept looking around themselves to check for attackers and avoided stepping on dry leaves.

Simultaneously, a few hundred metres ahead of them, in the royal dungeons below, a few guards gathered to rescue Vermish and Chooha. Their cries of help had alerted the royal ladybugs--who had summoned the additional guards. These bugs were the hand-maids of the princesses Squincy and Gnawcy. A few guards rescued the trapped mole-rats and helped clear the pests off their faces and bodies. The others ran after the Core Fulcrum.

"The cube relays SOS signals after every revolution around the garden. We should cover it quickly before someone notices them," said Vermish, relieved that his face was finally free of the painful crabs. "Let us put it back in the cage NOW."

All of them started running after the cube to capture it and place it in the cage. Ten guards approached the revolving cube in all directions, blocking its escape route, while two more pushed the wheeled-cage towards it. Just as they were about to capture it, the cube performed a surprising manoeuvre. When they lunged at it, it suddenly raised itself three feet above them. As a result, they dashed their heads together and collapsed in a painful heap.

"OW, my head hurts so badly," one said.

"Birds are chirping around mine," the second one said, touching his head.

"I am so dazed, I can hardly see anything," a third squealed.

The cube started revolving and emitting its SOS signals again, as earlier.

One guard had an idea and quickly disappeared down the corridor. He arrived with one more guard, carrying a large red carpet.

"This is one of the palace's old carpets. We can fling it over the cube and block its light," he said.

It is a very good idea, thought Chooha.

What an inane idea, thought the ladybugs, their eyes widened with shock.

To execute that idea, they had to all climb trees in the garden to a height above the revolving cube. One by one, each guard held one corner of the carpet and slowly climbed a tree. They did this until most of them balanced themselves precariously on trees, at a height above the revolving cube. The carpet spread out like a canopy above the garden, held by all the guards. Now they had to wait for the precise moment to drop it over the cube. If they committed any mistakes, they would have to start all over again. The ladybugs, exasperated by the absurdity of the guards, scurried off hurriedly to report the incident to the princesses in the palace.

Goldie slunk forward slowly, his head, shoulders and back lowered. Hisky, on the other side, reached the end of the clearing. Eight distinct, grass-laden paths lay ahead of them. The paths ended in a lawn hundred metres ahead. Behind the lawns, they could see some ruins and a domed structure, covered with thousands of glass bubbles. Those bubbles reflected the sky like a large bulging cluster of orbicular mirrors.

Interesting paths, thought Goldie, as he peered at the grass closely. The grass looked different, almost like the bristles of a large pipe-cleaner, and the rocks looked recently scrubbed clean. Why would anyone want to clean rocks? Maybe it had recently rained here, or maybe it had not, he thought.

"Which path should we take to the ruins?" he asked Professor Inabaox.

"Let me see now, the second one seems to be the shortest route. We should take that one."

As soon as Professor Inabaox turned around to instruct everyone to follow him down the path, Goldie saw some flashes of light emanating from the dome. The lights turned into tiny, cascading fireworks before disappearing. They had made no sound.

"Did you see that?" he shouted out to everyone. His voice echoed all around in the silence.

"See what?" Snowball and the others came bounding towards him.

"I saw red, blue, and green lights shooting up from the dome in the front. They turned into fireworks and then disappeared," Goldie pointed towards the dome.

Everyone stared at the dome for several minutes, but saw nothing remotely similar. All they saw were the thousands of reflections of the sky in the shiny bubbles.

"You must have imagined it," said Hisky. "Fatigue can get to you, you know."

"I wasn't imagining it --"

The ruins of Trapesky

"Then--where are those lights now? Why can't I see them?"

Goldie did not have an answer, but he was sure he hadn't imagined the lights.

"Let us explore the ruins. We may find some clues there," said Professor Inabaox, as he stepped on the path. The others followed him towards the ruins.

Below the dome, the guards were celebrating, as they had successfully covered the cube with the carpet. One guard had thrown the carpet at the cube with so much force that he had also landed on top of it. He had lain there, splayed on top, while the cube had continued its circular movement. After a few jittery moments, he had stood up and jumped off onto a tree, while the surrounding guards had laughed and cheered.

Now, they pulled the reluctant cube with the help of the carpet into the cage once more. The cage rose with the force of the cube and traversed with it. They caught the cage, forced it into a cell, and locked the cell. Happy at having successfully captured it, the guards cheered for each other as they made their way to the palace through the corridor. Vermish and Chooha felt so relieved, they wanted to throw a party. Little were they aware of the search party above them.

The *kitdents* followed Professor Inabaox down the chosen path until they reached the expansive lawn. They saw eight black toadstools arranged in two rows, in its centre: one row with larger toadstools, and the other one with smaller ones. The ruins and the domed structure flanked the lawn to the north, and a large well flanked the west side. They investigated around the well first. The mossy well had green, stagnant water, with steps going downwards along the wall, until the waterline. A bunch of daffodils grew on the bottom-most step and bobbed around in the breeze. It looked like an ordinary well. After exploring it, they walked towards the dome and circled around it a few times. They could neither see nor hear anything inside it. There seemed to be no one around. Hisky touched one of the glass bubbles on the dome out of curiosity, and his paw almost got stuck to it. He flinched and hurriedly withdrew his paw.

What was this coating on the dome made of? thought Hisky, as he looked at his paw, which still felt sticky. *Yuck!*

"This county also has not thrown us any clues so far--" the Professor said and continued when he saw the expression on Goldie's face, "--barring what Goldie claims he saw. The effects of the Valerian juice will wear out soon. We should return before we get caught by the mole-rats."

Disappointed, the *kitdents* turned around and started walking back to the bus. Tufty and Chaton, who were feeling fatigued by the activities of the day, sat down on the black toadstools to rest awhile. Suddenly, the ground below them started shaking, and an alarm rang out loudly.

"WHIRR! WHIRR! WHIRR! WHIRR! BONG! BONG! BONG! BONG!"

The startled *kitdents* started making a dash for the bus, bounding over the path to reach the clearing. However, the path did not co-operate. The eight paths rose vertically, threw the *kitdents* in the air and became giant legs. The legs seemed attached to the lawn, which got inflated to become a head, and the toadstools became its eyes.

It was a giant green spider and was over a hundred metres tall!

It moved its chelicerae menacingly at them as it lifted itself to its full height -- its entire body filling out. Shocked, they watched, as it raised one of its towering legs above Chaton -- who had fallen flat on the ground, to crush him. Snowball dashed forward and pulled him out of danger. The foot landed inches away from him with an earth-shattering BOOM. They darted and weaved around its legs to avoid getting crushed by the giant monster hot on their heels. Screeching loudly, it stalked them, trying to stamp them to death. At one point, the tip of Kuting's tail got crushed under the spider's leg, but he pulled it out, leaving a tuft of fur behind. As though the giant spider was not enough, scores of screeching mole-rat bandicoots jumped out of the well, brandishing spears and swords. A few of them even carried bows and arrows. They ran after the trespassers.

"SQUEAK! SQUEECH! KICH, KICH, KICH! Get those trespassing felids! They should not escape," they screeched loudly.

What were they doing in the well? How did they emanate from it? When they had checked it, there was no one there, Goldie thought.

Arrows started flying towards them. One of them grazed Professor Inabaox on his back, but he did not stop. Taking refuge behind a tree on the edge of the clearing, he elongated his claw to strike one guard--who squealed and fell on the ground. He repeated that exercise with two other guards--who also fell. Taking a cue from him, all the *kitdents* darted behind trees to shield themselves. The spider grew confused as it could not see the kittens from over the treetops. It stood in the clearing and turned its head around to locate them, its screams reverberating in the air. Taking advantage of the situation, Goldie, Snowball, Kattie and Tufty used their CLG shots to target one of the spider's legs each. Though they missed the first shot, they tried again. This time, all the shots found their mark, and the spider screamed in pain. Hisky, Ruffsaw, Salmonair and Kuting targeted the other four legs. They succeeded after two attempts each. In the meantime, Chaton, Seabreeze, Lemeow and Pilli joined the show-down with shots of their own. With each successful shot, they ran closer to the bus that began buzzing its wings to take off. After being shot in its legs several times, the spider lost control, staggered into the clearing and slammed to the ground, causing shock waves all around. One of its legs landed a few feet away from the bus. Alarmed birds flew out of the trees nearby, and debris scattered all around. The *kitdents* dashed towards the bus and boarded it one by one, their tails blowing behind them.

"Hurry!" said Professor Inabaox, as he helped them onboard quickly.

The attendants also gave them a hand.

The guards saw them boarding the bus and sped up their attack--while closing the gap between them. They threw spears at them--one of which hit the side of the dragonfly, piercing it. Bows and arrows filled the air like a swarm of bees and struck the bus. As the last *kitdent*, Pilli was boarding the bus, the dragonfly suddenly lifted off, leaving her hanging from its legs. Kattie bent to lift her up, when an arrow found her shoulder. She screamed, but did not let go of Pilli. The others helped lift her to safety. They shut all the doors and windows to prevent the arrows from flying inside. The attendants pulled out the arrow from Kattie's shoulder and nursed her wound. Luckily, the arrow's tip was not poisonous; she was safe. Professor Inabaox applauded her for her bravery. Everyone except Hisky, Ruffsaw, Kuting, and Salmonair cheered for her. As the dragonfly flew high in the air, they saw hundreds of mole-rat guards and soldiers gathered around the palace grounds and ruins. The king stood on the veranda in front of the palace and shook his fist at them. The princesses -- in their gaudy outfits -- standing next to the king, too yelled out profanities that no-one could understand, while several ladybugs fussed over them. Glad they were safe, the exhausted *kitdents* settled down in their seats to make the journey back.

When they reached the school, Goldie and Snowball pulled Kattie and Tufty into a private huddle and explained everything about the orb. They both agreed to join the twins as part of the square bond and agreed to meet them in the cactus garden after school hours to start the training. They were sure there would be no one there after dark. Hisky looked at them sharply as they huddled, as he knew they were up to something.

He had taken the book from the library to gain an advantage, but it had been a complete disappointment. It contained no important information about the Core Fulcrum except its history, followed by a paw-print and a silly poem which completely baffled him.

The poem is so cryptic; it makes no sense to me. Still, the book is safe in my possession and I will never return it. No one else will ever know the secrets either. Let them discuss and come up with pointless schemes. Yeah, he thought.

CHAPTER ELEVEN

The Square Bond

Clawcia wondered where the four members of her group had disappeared, since she had not seen them since morning. She was at art class and had made a cut-out of a cat. She had also designed various accessories for it. Her cat was a fluffy, blue-and-silver Nebelung cat, with a large pink bow. Pompom helped her in the activity and cut out all the accessories. The accessories were: heart-shaped sunglasses and a pink purse. Professor Kitwalk walked around the classroom to look at what everyone had made.

"All right, looks like everyone has completed the work," she clapped. "Please walk to the front with your partners -- one team at a time, with your creations. When I call out your names, please take your cat cut-out and place it in front of the animation projector. It will be fun," she said, delighted.

"Cica and Grimis," called Professor Kitwalk.

The duo walked to the front holding the cut-out of a tabby-coated, short-furred Abyssinian cat. It was slim and tall and wore a hat. They placed in front of the animation projector and stood next to it. Professor Kitwalk turned the projector on, so that the spotlight fell on the cut-out, and set the mode to 'cat-walk'.

"Each drawing, each piece of art has a personality, and this projector helps bring that personality to life," she said and clicked on the start button.

As the projector began to whirr, the slim, tabby cat sprang to life, swishing its tail. It sashayed to the front gracefully in a straight line, struck a pose and blinked its green eyes at the audience. There were loud cheers from everyone. After they changed the cat's accessories, it repeated the cat-walk with a different style of strutting and struck a different pose. The applause was even louder this time.

"Meow, purr," it said with happiness, blinking its lashes.

"Very good *kitdents*. Now Clawcia and Pompom, please proceed to the front of the class. Let us see what your cat can do," Professor Kitwalk instructed. The Abyssinian cat turned back into a cut-out. Spotlight was important for an extraordinary existence.

Clawcia and Pompom placed their cut-out in the centre of the spotlight as instructed and stepped aside. Professor Kitwalk set the mode to 'dance' this time.

The cat sprang to life as soon as the music began. The song was, 'Dance little lady dance', and it danced to its tunes, swaying, spinning, jumping, sliding, and boogying its way through the song gracefully. Cheers erupted as it finished with a flip and a split on the floor as the song ended. It stayed there panting as the claps resounded in the room.

"Encore, encore," they cried.

After all of them completed demonstrations with their cut-outs, Professor Kitwalk repeated the exercise in a group. She changed modes, and they changed their actions in response. The final group-dance was the best, and the most synchronised one Clawcia had ever seen. They clapped hard as it ended.

"Now you understand why this is important? I am hoping we will win the gold medal for the cat-walk, dance, and choreography events during the next Kitaganza competition. It takes the best designs and co-ordinated choreography to achieve the top spot. Looking at your work today, I have the full confidence that you are one of the best. You need to practise cat-walking and dancing with your cut-outs. During the next session, we should try that, along with some art-work for sets."

Everyone thought it would be fun to dance with their cut-outs. Once the session ended, they stored their art-work in cupboards, milled out of the art-room cheerfully and returned to the main classroom on the same floor for the next session on N-Counters.

Just as Clawcia approached the classroom, she saw Billy walking towards it, with a guitar strapped over his back.

"Hi Clawcia, have you seen the bunch?" he asked, humming a tune to himself.

"No, I haven't seen them the whole day today," she responded. She wished she could show her cut-out to Billy and maybe it would dance to a song his group played.

Goldie, Snowball, Kattie, and Tufty took the elevator, rushing into the classroom to see Clawcia, Melowflues, and Billy, deeply engaged in a conversation. Melowflues giggled as usual, conversing in her high-pitched, sing-song voice.

"Where have you all been? What happened to you Kattie?" asked Clawcia when she saw them -- looking more maroon than usual.

"Secret mission; -- I am fine," said Kattie, touching the bandage on her shoulder.

"Did you find it?" asked Billy, with a twinkle in his eye.

"You heard the lady -- secret mission," said Goldie and winked.

Snowball patted Billy on his back and sat down at the desk next to him. Shortly afterwards, all the other classmates entered the classroom, followed by the professor.

Professor Manimore patiently waited for all the *kitdents* to settle down and began. She walked to the front of the classroom and faced them.

"Last time I had asked the class a riddle. Was anyone able to solve it?"

Cica raised her hand.

"Please tell me the solution, Cica."

"Ma'am, the answer is '1', '5' and '8'."

"Very good! That is correct. Could you tell the class how you solved it?"

"The first clue is that the product of their ages is forty. There are six unique ways in which we can arrive at that product: one -- '1x1x40', two -- '1x2x20', three -- '1x4x10', four -- '1x5x8', five -- '2x2x10' and six -- '2x4x5'. The second clue is that the sum of their ages is half of the cat's age. However, the friend still cannot solve it because there are over two combinations that add up-to the clue. The two combinations that have the same sum are: '1+5+8' and '2+2+10'. Both add up to fourteen. The friend still cannot guess the answer. The last clue is that the youngest kitten likes cheesecake. That rules out the '2', '2' and '10' combination giving the final answer of '1', '5' and '8'." Cica said triumphantly.

"Very well done Cica. You deserve applause from all of us and this special marble." Professor Manimore rewarded her efforts with a magical, floating marble.

The class clapped for her as she beamed and accepted it. Professor Manimore continued teaching them other concepts like geometrical shapes for the next hour. She used pliable glass to create different shapes and wrote all measurements using temporary markers on the surfaces. Once the class ended, she compressed the pliable glass into a marble and dropped it into her bag. After that, they were free to leave for the day.

Billy, Clawcia and Melowflues wished their friends the best-of-luck and left. Goldie, Snowball, Kattie and Tufty grabbed their bags and headed towards the rear of the school buildings -- towards the cactus garden, on the right side of the kitchen. They looked around to make sure they were not being followed and bounded to the rear. The cactus garden contained a wooden shack all the way behind for all the gardening tools. Though there were cupboards all around, there was ample space in the centre of the room. As expected, there was no one around. All the classes in the kitchen took place in the mornings. They entered the shack and bolted the door behind them to sit down comfortably in the centre. Goldie removed the book from his bag as the others curiously bent forward in anticipation.

Far up in the school building, Hisky, Kuting, Salmonair and Ruffsaw removed their binoculars and kept them in their bags.

"Didn't I tell you there were planning something?" said Hisky.

"We should follow them and find out what they are doing in the cactus garden," said Kuting.

"Why bother? Let them do whatever they want to. I want to go home now," said Ruffsaw. Salmonair agreed with him. As they were responsible senior *kitdents*, they did not want to get involved in nefarious activities.

"I will go with you Kuting. If we learn something interesting, we will let you both know," Hisky said to Salmonair and Ruffsaw. He badly wanted a partner. His two other gang members Gattino and Mewtiony were not part of this course.

"That is fine with us. All the best," said Ruffsaw and left the room.

Before Salmonair left, he placed two brown pellets in Hisky's paw.

"Here, you might need these. Use them wisely. However, do nothing that contradicts the NDA, or you will get into serious trouble. Also, be careful, this is a small dose and works only for ten minutes," he said and departed.

Salmonair accompanied Ruffsaw to the school parking ground. They were just in time to catch their school buses home. Salmonair sat in the fish bus and Ruffsaw in the beaver one. Hisky stared at the pellets, wondering what they were. Then in the next moment he had an epiphany and smiled. Kuting and he took the elevators down to head towards the cactus garden.

In the shack, the four held each other's paws, forming a square. Goldie pressed the metallic paw-print, and immediately, the orb started forming around them. Soon they were all seated in baskets, bobbing gently on one side. Dr. Diadoms' training session began.

When the face appeared, Kattie and Tufty got initially startled as the twins had expected, but soon got used to it.

"Welcome again, *kitdents*. I am so glad to meet you again. Now I see that there are four of you. That you were all engulfed by the orb is proof that you are all enlightened beings," said Dr. Diadoms.

"Yes Dr. Diadoms," they said together and nodded.

"Before beginning the lessons, I would like to first get the square bond formed to ensure that none of you will use the powers for the wrong purpose. Please form a circle while holding paws and close your eyes. You will neither feel nor hear anything." When they followed his instructions, he closed his eyes and chanted a mantra. Four distinct wisps of light that look like teardrops emanated from the top of the orb. One drop fell on each of their heads and got absorbed. The very next moment, an electric current emanated from their ears and connected with the current from all other kittens', until the connections looked like a square with diagonals, when viewed from the top. The square bond was complete. "You may now open your eyes and relax in your baskets. I will begin my narration," he said. They relaxed once more in their baskets as the audio and video streaming started, and the orb screen sprang to life in dazzling colours. Kattie and Tufty were glad they had agreed. They were thoroughly enjoying themselves.

The orb started playing visuals of the four scientists in the cave, on the island, in the middle of the caldera, on top of the dormant volcano, in the middle of the big, Thacar desert, working with small pieces of the ore, from which they had extracted the Core Fulcrum. because of the properties of the gem, their physical abilities drastically changed. They now bounded from tree-to-tree like agile primates and climbed vertical surfaces. They built tree houses on the top of tall trees and resided in them. Dr. Diadoms created the design of the new Egytica, a haven comprising tree houses, hovering vehicles, and other fantastic structures. Their testing was almost complete. The next step was to take the technology to the masses. That is when disaster struck, and the canids attacked Egytica. The visuals showed the horrifying details of the war that ensued. Egytica, with its simple sandstone structures could not resist the external forces. The canids defeated the much weaker felids with ease. During the ensuing war, they tore apart families and burned magnificent structures in Egytica to the ground. The monarch King Skatzer and the inhabitants of his kingdom fled as soon as possible. Kattie had tears in her eyes when the visuals ended.

"When they kidnapped the king's daughter, I introduced the cube to him and his council members to enhance their powers so they could fight back and rescue her. Once I showed him the powers, he wanted me to help the masses too. So, I did, and the rest is history," Dr. Diadoms continued.

Tufty clapped his paws when he finished the story.

"Today I will start the training about your basic powers and how to enhance them using the Core Fulcrum. Please understand that before the discovery of the Core Fulcrum, felids had no powers. They were intelligent but could not jump high or climb trees. Their vision was nothing extraordinary, because of which they were easy to capture. After the discovery of the special ore, all the felids inherited three basic powers from their ancestors: the power of agility and flexibility, the power of balance and the power of night vision. Some felids could climb trees, and others couldn't, but they were still very strong and agile. We needed to train them to enhance these basic powers." Dr. Diadoms paused, checking if they had questions.

"So, you're saying that all of us have these basic powers, but not the enhanced ones, am I right?" asked Kattie.

"And if the Core Fulcrum gets destroyed, we will lose even those basic powers. We are who we are because the Core Fulcrum protects us," said Goldie.

Kattie and Tufty widened their eyes when the full realisation hit them. They hadn't realised Professor

Inabaox was talking about all their basic survival instincts.

"Right," Dr. Diadoms said.

Outside, Hisky and Kuting had slinked into the cactus garden unseen by anyone. They laid low on the ground and moved forward towards the shack that was throwing unusual shadows around. Once they reached the shack, they peered through the cracks and saw a big rainbow-coloured, swirling, opaque sphere in the room. They could see no one else there. Hisky almost fell backwards in surprise.

Something has happened to Goldie and his friends. No matter how much I would like them to disappear, I did not expect it to happen so soon; he thought. *Has the sphere engulfed them?* He almost had second thoughts about continuing his spying, but wanted to unearth the truth. He swallowed one pellet and gave one to Kuting, who also swallowed it. Instantly, they got absorbed into the wooden wall of the shack until they were part-and-parcel of it. They could see and hear everything, but they could not move out of their state. They heard a voice talking. It said,

"To enhance those basic powers, you need to stand in front of the Core Fulcrum. You cannot inherit enhanced powers; you need to gain them with vigorous training. Keep the Core Fulcrum in front of you and touch your right paw on its top surface. Keep it that way for five seconds. Your powers will get enhanced and will remain enhanced forever."

To Hisky's shock, next he heard Snowball's voice from inside the sphere. *He was alive! This sphere had not killed them!*

Hisky and Kuting Snoop outside the shack

Snowball said, "Could you please let us know more about the enhanced basic powers? What are the differences between those and the basic powers?".

Curiouser and curiouser, Hisky thought.

Kuting almost fainted in his 'wooden' state. He felt claustrophobic for the first time in his life. He urgently wanted to use the litter box enclosure.

"With enhanced powers, you can jump distances that are a hundred times over normal and climb vertical surfaces up-to a hundred times your height. The only way you can die is through a Valerian laser shot, as I mentioned in the previous session. You have nine lives but with enhanced powers, it's almost impossible to lose even one. Night vision changes to X-ray vision, which means, you can see through objects. However, you can use this power only at night," he said.

That answer seemed to satisfy the kittens, and they discussed amongst themselves about this new-found knowledge.

"Any more questions?" asked Dr. Diadoms.

"I have one question unrelated to this lesson," said Goldie.

"Go ahead."

"Does the Core Fulcrum ever shoot out rays of light on its own?"

"Hm, it could if it believes its end is near, but..." he said and hesitated for a long time. He started looking around the room with an uneasy look on his old face.

"Go on Dr. Diadoms. Please tell us more," urged Goldie.

"I would, if not for the intruder in the room. We are not alone... I cannot continue," Dr. Diadoms said.

Intruder? Goldie thought, with a rising sense of alarm.

"Exit rainbow rondure," said Snowball immediately.

Dr. Diadoms disappeared, followed by the orb, and they fell softly on the wooden floor. The remaining wisps got absorbed by the book. Goldie quickly put the book back in his bag.

They started searching around the room for the intruder. They looked under and around cupboards but could find no one. Tufty opened the door and checked all around the shack too but found nothing unusual. He came back inside to tell them the coast was clear.

"Maybe it was just a passing bat or an insect," said Tufty.

"Yes, there is no intruder here," said Snowball.

"Hmm -- I find it hard to believe that Dr. Diadoms was wrong. There must have been someone," said Goldie.

"The intruder must have left by now. Let us also get out of here. It is already late, and I need to reach home soon, or my mother will scold me," said Kattie, feeling anxious.

Just as they were about to give up, they heard a moan from the wall next to the entrance door. The 'wall' started peeling off until two kitten-shaped planks fell on the floor in front of them with a plunk. The wooden layer on top of the fallen planks slowly vanished to reveal Hisky and Kuting! All of them could only watch in disbelief. They had seen nothing like this before.

* * *

CHAPTER TWELVE

Detention for the
Manzar Twins

When Hisky and Kuting recovered, they confronted Goldie and the others.

"What was that sphere all about? Who were you talking to?" asked Hisky.

"They were talking to someone called Dr. Diadoms. I heard Goldie addressing 'the voice' with that name," said Kuting, pointing his toe accusingly at all of them.

"Shan't tell you anything," said Goldie defiantly.

"Give me that book," demanded Hisky.

"Take a walk," said Goldie, turning to run out.

"Grreowww!" said Hisky and grabbed Goldie's bag, attempting to take it away from him forcibly. Snowball punched him hard on the face, and Hisky staggered backward. Kuting bit Snowball's arm, so Tufty yanked him away with his tail. Kattie also join the fight by hitting Hisky with her bag several times -- who turned around and scratched her wounded shoulder with his claws, because of which the bandage came off. The wound started oozing blood again.

"Ouch!" she screamed, staggering backward.

Goldie was so angered by Hisky's actions that he hissed and slammed his head into Hisky's abdomen, sending him crashing into a cupboard.

"MeOOWW," Hisky said, touching the back of his head where it hit the cupboard.

The brawl continued for a few more minutes, with all of them scratching, spitting, hitting, hissing and yowling until they defeated the two intruders. Hisky and Kuting lay on the floor, clutching their abdomens, writhing in pain.

"Come on, let's go," said Goldie finally, wiping the blood off his chin where Hisky had bitten him. Tufty was missing a 'tuft' of fur from his back where Kuting had scratched him. Snowball was the only one left unscathed.

They took the snail bus home as it was one of the few buses plying after school hours. As they travelled home, they discussed the intrusion and wondered how Hisky had merged with wood. They never knew a transformation like that was possible. A senior had helped them for sure. Goldie and Snowball dropped Kattie home at Shimmering Streams before they reached their house. It was well past dinnertime by the time they reached. Niamy and Paka were not happy with their late appearance, as they pushed their way through the kitten-door but the twins provided a satisfactory explanation.

The next morning, Professor Inabaox summoned Goldie and Snowball to the staff room. Hisky stood there with bandages all over this body and glared at them. They knew what was coming.

"What were you doing in the garden shack after school hours?" Professor Inabaox asked. He noticed the bandage on Goldie's chin.

"We were practising, sir--" blurted Snowball.

"Practising what?"

"A dance and a play, sir," said Snowball, remembering the conversation with Clawcia the previous day.

Hisky looked at him incredulously.

"He is lying, sir!" he said.

Professor Inabaox put his paw on his mouth to ask Hisky to be quiet while he continued to question the Manzar twins.

"Why were you practising a dance and a play in the shack?"

"Clawcia--our friend is working on a sequence for the next Kitaganza, and we wanted to help her. It was a surprise for her. To keep it a surprise, we had to... um... find a private place," said Snowball.

Goldie hung his head and nodded.

"Hmm..." said Professor Inabaox, not entirely convinced, "Why did you hit Hisky and Kuting?"

"They interrupted and disturbed us," continued Snowball. "They also grabbed our bags."

"Is that true Hisky? Did you grab their bags?"

"Yes, but--"

Professor Inabaox gives them detention

"That is enough. I don't know who started this fight and who ended it. I am assigning detention for all of you. I don't want any *kitdents* getting into scuffles on the school premises. This afternoon, the three of you will proceed to the marble room for thirty minutes. I repeat, we *do not allow* violence on the school premises," he signed on the paper and handed it to the flustered class teacher, Professor Neko, who led them to the marble room.

There was no mention of the book, the orb or the 'wood' incident. The professor probably knew but did not want to focus on those aspects. He probably believed that as enlightened *kitdents*, they had the right to access informative material. Goldie wondered about the method that Hisky had used to merge with wood. He was sure there was a senior who had helped him. Hisky was still unaware that his book was a copy. He believed the Manzar twins had laid their hands on another special book. He hadn't quite seen the title of the book as Goldie had put it away in his bag.

The detention marble room was a spherical room at the top of the school that turned around the whole day in all directions. At a height of four feet, the marble room was not very tall, but that wasn't a reason to celebrate. Since it was full of marbles, it was uncomfortable to roll inside it. Some marbles could hurt.

"Ow, wow, ow," said Hisky as he fell on the bed of marbles from the ceiling of the sphere.

"Ew, not my mouth," said Snowball, spitting a marble out.

"Ew, ew, meow," said Goldie, as he slid and skated on the marbles before losing balance. A deluge of marbles landed on his body.

They tossed and turned, skated and spun around, while marbles hit them from all directions. It felt similar to being inside a washing machine without the water. It was not a pleasant experience. Goldie decided never to use the book in school. It was just too risky.

During the next class -- which was for Languages, Goldie and Snowball told Clawcia about their 'skit story' to Professor Inabaox. She was shocked but promised to support them in case anyone asked her about it.

Goldie scolded Snowball for lying.

"Why did you have to cook up such a random story about dancing? You know I have two left feet."

"What did you expect me to say? Sir, we were learning about the Secrets of the Core Fulcrum inside a rainbow-coloured orb with Dr. Diadoms. We stopped when he announced an intruder and then saw Hisky and Kuting literally fall out as wooden planks from the wall. Would that have been better?"

Goldie saw his point but was still not happy about him lying.

"Do not lie again -- or I will have to tell Dad. Even though you lied, the consequence was the same. It would have been better to have said you were reading a book about the Core Fulcrum," he said. Snowball looked away, miffed with him.

This whole detention episode had deflated Goldie's spirits for the day. He continued working on the grammar exercise Professor Neko had given them, but badly needed a fresh walk to mull things over.

In the meantime, a thousand miles north of Mew Scape -- at Trapesky's royal palace, King Koresque was not happy. Several aspects worried him: the evil felids had almost found the Core Fulcrum -- although the guards mentioned that they did not discover the secret entrance, and the development of the city of Vamoush was behind schedule. He had paid the architects an advance of several tons of golden-meat coins. They were now asking for more.

"Your highness. We need the additional coins to build the secret traps and conduits you told us about in the previous review session," Alaksnar, the chief architect said. "Now that you have that special gem in your possession, you would need the best protection in the entire world. The original list of traps is no longer enough. Trust me -- I have been long associated with your dynasty and I care about your satisfaction," he repeated with false concern. He was the slyest murid in the whole of Murid-land.

"Take the coins but complete the construction by next week. We cannot afford to delay any more," King Koresque said. He planned to move the Core Fulcrum to the new city once readied.

The cube had left a trace of star dust wherever they had taken it. With great difficultly he had got the surroundings cleaned up with the spider's venom because water had not worked. On a whim, he had tried cleaning the traces with venom and it had shown positive results. They had a huge storage tank of venom extracted from arachnids inhabiting the kingdom. They used the venom to lace their battle weapons. With the help from his guards, he had removed all other signs like flattened grass and shrubs too. It had been almost impossible to clean up the interior passages of the royal dungeons because of poor lighting and its uneven, mossy surfaces. If the felids discovered the entrance to the dungeons from the well, the signs would lead them to it. The glittery, enamelled walls of Vamoush would offer a good camouflage -- until they found the Pivot. After they destroyed the cube with the Pivot, they would attack the evil felids. A son would avenge his father's death.

After Professor Neko's session was over, Goldie headed out for a walk. Snowball still miffed with him, stayed back to spend time with Billy, Kattie, Clawcia and Melowflues. Billy and Melowflues had composed a new tune and were keen to play it in front of their friends. Hisky was in too much pain to bother about their activities. He felt frustrated because he could not explain the situation to Gattino and Mewtiony. Tufty saw Goldie leave the classroom and bounded after him. He caught up with him as he reached the ground floor.

"What's up Gold? You look down. Everything ok?" he asked, gently butting his head against Goldie's shoulder.

"I am fine -- really I am. I have just been mulling over the events since yesterday. Although we could not trace the Core Fulcrum, I have a strong hunch it is in Trapesky. I cannot get the lights I saw out of my mind," Goldie said, walking towards the lawn near the fountains.

"But Professor Inabaox will not take us there again. He feels the cube is not there, and that Trapesky is too dangerous."

"If he doesn't agree, I will go there on my own."

Tufty stopped walking and stared at Goldie, shocked.

"You must be joking --"

"No -- I am not. I am truly convinced that the Core Fulcrum is there. We have to retrieve it, whether no one else accompanies us."

"I would like to go with you -- but how? None of the buses will transport us without either Professor Quemarke or Professor Inabaox's permission."

"Then, we will have to borrow one and manoeuvre it ourselves."

"No -- Goldie, not that option. Why don't we talk to Professor Inabaox again? He too wants the Core Fulcrum back."

Goldie thought for some time and then agreed.

"Okay, but if he doesn't agree, you know what we should do," he said.

Tufty agreed.

By that time, they had entered the lawn beside the science labs and started walking on the surrounding path.

There was one *kitdent* seated on a bench, busy reading. Tufty recognised him as Mawgix -- the senior who had lent the slate to him. Mawgix was a tall, black-and-gold, short-furred slim cat.

"Hi Mawgix, how are you?" said Tufty to the senior who looked up at him.

"Hi there Tufty, I am well, how are you?"

"Not too bad. Let me introduce you to my friend, Goldie."

"Hi Mawgix, thank you so much for lending the slate to us the other day," said Goldie.

"You're most welcome. That is what seniors are for -- to give a hand. Hope it was useful," Mawgix said.

"The most useful so far -- cannot thank you enough," said Goldie.

"Heh heh. By the time you reach the tenth grade, you have a lot of tricks up your sleeve... um... arm. Do not hesitate if you need my help with anything," the senior cat said.

"Actually, I need your help with something else. I need information about something."

"Sure, just ask."

"Do you know of any substance that can turn a kitten into wood?"

"Hmm. I think powder made with the bark of a Neem tree can do that. I would need to check with my batch mates -- who specialize in that subject."

Aha, thought Goldie. *One senior had helped Hisky.*

"Are there other such ingredients that can turn you into a different non-living object?"

"There is a course called 'Natural Transformations' -- a field that Professor Quemarke specializes in. It is an optional subject for the tenth graders."

"Would you know any tenth grader who has chosen that optional subject?"

"Yes -- Salmonair and Seabreeze."

Now it all made sense to Goldie. Salmonair had helped Hisky. He wondered whether Dr. Diadoms covered the same subject during the 'Secrets of the Core Fulcrum' express training. They would find out.

"If you don't mind, could you please tell us your optional subject?"

"Sure; -- it's 'Digital Interfaces'. It is all about decoding various objects we see around us: both inanimate and living, and creating digital algorithms to interact with them. One example is a slate. Its reflective surface can store information. Another example is a universal communicator and translator. We all know that a universal translator already exists, one that can understand communication from all living things and convert those signals to a language that we can understand. I am working on a project called Universal Action Controller or the UAC. I am attempting to do something for the first time. Using the UAC, not only can we communicate with all objects but can control its actions. Yesterday, I could make a snail turn away from its favourite food, even though it was moving toward it initially. This is under testing. In fact, as we speak, I am writing a thesis about this topic."

Mawgix's project awed Goldie and Tufty. It sounded very 'cool' and powerful. He promised to let them try it once his testing was over--which delighted them both. After speaking to him about his thesis for a few more minutes, they left the garden and walked to the lab where Professor Ensure would conduct the first lesson in science. He wanted to teach them how to create ghosts out of simple ingredients. *That sounded scary*.

CHAPTER THIRTEEN

Ghosts and Defence Arts

Joybob and Trixy reached the spot from where they had stolen the Core Fulcrum. There were many more robotic guards around this time, and the alarm-system wires they had gnawed through a few days earlier looked resurrected -- sealed in a glass case.

They climbed a tree to get a better look, but everything looked covered up.

Bummer! How would they enter the compound this time? Joybob grew anxious.

They did not have information regarding the location of the Pivot. They had reached the location of the Core Fulcrum, by following the president of Lussian Peak -- hitching a ride onto his jet plane. As spies permanently posted at Lussian peak, it was their job to follow their most high-ranked enemies.

One of them will know the location of the Pivot. It will definitely slip during their conversations in the ensuing days. Stalking them is the only option. There were only seven more days to go before we face the gallows, thought Trixy.

At Meow Wow High School, the fifth-graders were in the science lab. Professor arranged the containers with the ingredients in front of himself. He placed broken shell flakes, soap base, chalk dust, baking soda, glue, water, and special glitter next to the induction cooker. There were several glass tubes, beakers and other apparatus also on his table. Each *kitdent* had their own table with ingredients and equipment on it for the lab work.

"All right, take this medium-sized beaker and put thirty grams (one ounce) of the soap base into it. Keep it on the induction flame for warming. Set the temperature to a hundred-and-forty-degrees Fahrenheit. Keep the tweezers handy since the beaker will become hot."

The *kitdents* followed his instructions.

"Please take another bowl and mix the shell flakes, chalk dust, baking soda and glue in it until it's a gooey mass. Add two tablespoons of water and mix again."

There was a lot clinking around the room as everyone mixed the ingredients.

"Now, using the tweezers, hold the beaker and pour the melted soap base into the bowl with the gooey mass. Mix well."

When they followed his instructions, the white-coloured mass started bubbling slowly.

"Next, take a mould of any shape and coat it with this special glitter. Be careful not to put too much glitter. Just a pinch is enough."

Everyone took the glitter out of the bottle and sprinkled it on the moulds they had selected. Hisky had the mould of a horse, Goldie -- a rabbit, Snowball -- a jellyfish, Kattie -- an eagle, Billy -- a fish, Gattino -- a cat and so on... Gattino sprinkled with so much force that the lid came off, and a heaped tablespoonful of glitter fell into the mould. He hurriedly took out as much as he could, but the wastage could not be reversed.

"Now, slowly pour the bubbling, gooey mixture into the mould and stand back, as the mixture can splash into your eyes," said the professor, as he poured the mixture into a mould shaped like a mouse.

They waited for a few seconds but nothing happened. The mixture reacted and bubbled slowly. Just as they were giving up, Kattie's white eagle floated up and started flying around slowly. She clapped with glee. Similarly, all other moulds came to life and floated around. The *kitdents* clapped and rejoiced when they saw the slimy ghosts hovering around. Gattino kept staring at his mould as it bubbled for a longer time than expected. Suddenly, the slippery blob from his cat-shaped mould shot upwards with its mouth open and its teeth bared. It truly looked like a sinister ghost.

"Gattino, watch out! Looks like you put too much magic glitter!" said the professor, but it was too late.

The ghost launched itself onto Snowball and threw a small ball of slime into his eyes before flying out of the window, cackling wickedly as it went. A trace of vanishing sparkly dust trailed behind it. Snowball meowed in pain and rushed to the basin to wash his eyes. Gattino stared at Snowball incredulously. Everyone's jaws were almost on the floor. *What was that?*

Professor Ensure creates the ghost of a mouse

"All, you unfortunately just witnessed the formation of an actual ghost," the professor explained.

"What? Where did it go?" asked Goldie.

"Is it dangerous?" asked Hisky.

There were several simultaneous questions.

"I am afraid, it has fled to Ghastly Catyons -- a haunted town inhabited by all the ghosts of Eartavista. Most of them are not dangerous, but a few can cause great harm."

By then, most of the other ghosts started popping like bubbles and disappeared into thin air.

"Are we allowed to go to there to see them?" asked Cica.

"No. No. Why on earth would you want to risk your life? Though most of them are only pests -- who will prank you all the time, there are a few that are dangerous."

Snowball was not happy about being the first victim of a prank. Cica thought it sounded interesting.

Professor Hisstoly's class had started in the room next to theirs. He wore robes that looked like the ones they found in ancient books. The whole class looked like a set from Cantialand, a county from the far northwest. Katzchen stood in front, reading out the history of the Sphynx cat -- a breed with almost no fur. It had large ears and sometimes had a fine growth of fur resembling chamois. A family of Sphynx cats enacted a scene next to him. They pranced about playing different roles. These cats were obviously just animated versions. Hirra and Yavru sat in the front and took down notes. Goldie was not very fond of Lineage as a subject, since it required one to remember so many dates and events by-heart. However, Snowball was very curious about the different breeds and their evolution.

Professor Inabaox started the Curiosity class next door by listing all the achievements of the search operation. Then, he listed out all those aspects of it, where they had achieved little success.

"I will start off by saying that you all did very well – especially given the fact that you had almost no training. However, some situations we encountered took us by surprise and highlighted our lack of preparation. After an urgent conference with Professor Quemarke and President Skailimet, we have decided we should train you in Defence Arts. We will attempt another search and rescue operation soon. This timely training will prepare you for all the dangers you may encounter."

"Sir, what areas will we explore this time? Will we go back to the counties we visited?" asked Chaton.

"No. We have concluded that the Core Fulcrum is not in those five counties near Mew Scape. We will have to try our luck with other ones. I am waiting for the list from the ministry."

Goldie thought of talking to Professor Inabaox after the session to convince him otherwise. With Dr. Diadoms' confirmation, he felt his hunch was right.

"Let me introduce these two young martial artists -- Kusti and Kedi. They will conduct the session today and will teach you some important defence techniques. I have an important meeting with Professor Quemarke, hence I will leave you in their honourable company," said Professor Inabaox and departed.

Kusti was a short, fat, brown-coloured cat, and Kedi was a slim, beige-coloured one. They both had very thin tails and spoke with a strange accent alluding to the fact that they were not from any neighbouring county.

"We need three pairs of volunteers to show three basic defence techniques. Kedi will be my opponent, and we will take turns attacking and defending. We will show the techniques first, then the volunteers can try them out," Kusti said. "We use the first technique when the fight is between two opponents in the same medium: air-air, land-land, water-water. We use the second technique for a fight between opponents in two different mediums: air-land, air-water and so on... We use the third technique for a fight between two opponents, when either of them is invisible. We call them the SM, DM, and IM defence techniques respectively. We use these techniques with a combination of different weapons for the enhancement of self-defence, which we will show you. Who will volunteer for the first technique, also known as the SM?"

Ruffsaw and Seabreeze volunteered. They drank a few drops of Valerian juice offered by the instructors. The instructors showed the volunteers a sequence of moves to help them aim better with their weapons and overpower an opponent that was dangerously close. In the same medium, the plane of vision was much clearer, so the confrontation had to be quick and direct. Ruffsaw and Seabreeze followed the demonstrations precisely and nailed the block, strike, and tumble techniques. Everyone applauded when they completed their demonstration.

The next two volunteers were Pilli and Tufty for the DM techniques. Kusti told them how to use stealth when the opponent was not entirely visible. Both the instructors then showed them a few instruments like the inter-medium listening buds that they could use to listen to auditory changes in other mediums around them, and the binoculars, which they were already familiar with. First Pilli flew in the air using motorised wings, while Tufty fought her from the floor. Tufty performed the elastic-lasso pull with his rear leg perfectly to bring Pilli down, and she elongated her claw in defence. Next, it was Tufty's turn to fly, and Pilli's turn to fight from the floor. Tufty elongated his claws to attack her, but she created a shield by spinning her paws rapidly. The claw bounced back and retracted itself. She immediately performed the lasso trick and brought him down. There were hoots, cheers and claps all around after the successful demonstration.

"Well done, Pilli!" shouted Kattie.

"Super tackle Tufty," cried Goldie from the back.

For a change, even Hisky, Kuting and Ruffsaw cheered for them -- which was an unusual occurrence.

The next and last demonstration was for the IM technique. Ironically, Goldie and Hisky volunteered at the same time. Snowball tried to discourage Goldie since he had a bruise, but he sped ahead, ignoring his protests. Hisky was waiting for this opportunity. They both drank Valerian juice first, eyeing each other venomously. Hisky was itching to use his claws. The instructors showed them some interesting gadgets for self-defence during such encounters. They gave the kittens a thermal patch to detect the heat from an invisible opponent and special goggles to detect infrared light. Kusti taught them how to elongate their legs behind to kick backwards, to spin around fast (like a top) and to flip in the air. They practised those moves for some time and signalled when they were ready to start. They both wore thermal patches and goggles to prepare for their tussle.

After that, Kedi gave Hisky a small purple-coloured pellet. They had made this pellet by mixing Aloe-Vera pulp, juice from the Java-plum fruit, and a special powder. The effect of the pellet would last for three minutes. As soon as he swallowed the pellet, Hisky started becoming invisible in parts, with hilarious effects. First his legs disappeared, leaving just his body and face visible. Then, his twitching nose disappeared, followed by his shoulders, forehead, ears and eyes. His abdomen, eyebrows, tail, and mouth were the last to disappear. The *kitdents* tried to suppress their laughter but couldn't, and burst out laughing. Goldie stifled a grin, but felt his senses heighten, because he knew Hisky would not spare any punches against him.

He felt his back heating and quickly turned to face him, but got punched in his left shoulder. The blow caused him to tumble backwards and fall on the floor. He saw Hisky's infrared outline above him as he tried to get up, but Hisky punched him harder this time on his cheek. Blood oozed into his mouth as his tooth cut into his cheek. As he watched, Hisky jumped high in the air to land on Goldie's abdomen, but Goldie rolled over just in time. Hisky instead landed on the floor. Before he could get up, Goldie spun around fast and collided with him. Hisky crashed into the front board and the duster fell on the floor. Hisky retaliated by elongating his claw and scratched Goldie on his left rear leg. Blood trickled from the cut. He winced and took a step backward, crashing into the wall behind. A poster fell from the wall because of the impact. All the other *kitdents* who were watching could not see Hisky but were aghast at the sight of falling objects.

The instructors also grew uneasy at the sight of a fight that did not look 'playful'. They were glad when the invisibility wore off, and Hisky became visible in parts again, with equally hilarious effects. This time, it was Goldie's turn to become invisible; he swallowed the proffered pellet quickly. He became invisible a lot more quickly and uniformly, his whole body faded into thin air in a few moments. Hisky looked very nervous because he knew it was pay-back time for Goldie. He was right. Goldie launched at attack on him before he could react. He used all the manoeuvres that the instructors had taught and did not give Hisky a chance to strike back. Hisky lashed his paws randomly in the air and tried to shield his face. Everyone watched as he flipped a few times in the air to avoid Goldie's blows. Finally, he fell on the floor -- dazed, when Goldie punched him hard and pinned him down. The instructors blew a whistle as soon as Goldie became visible. Everyone cheered hard. It had been an entertaining show.

"Ahem, good, but when you are practising, you should not use your full force -- no one needs to tell you that," said Kusti, glaring at both of them.

Kedi handed over medicated swabs to both of them to wipe their bruises. Snowball felt proud of Goldie and patted him on his back. The instructors then made everyone practise the techniques one-by-one until everyone understood them well. They needed to practise every day to become experts, as knowledge was not enough.

***

CHAPTER FOURTEEN

The Tunnel Garden

After the session was complete, Goldie, Snowball, and Tufty went to the staff room to find Professor Inabaox. Kattie stayed back to talk to Clawcia about her cut-out for the Kitaganza. As Goldie and the gang reached the staff room, they saw other teachers there -- either working on their own or in deep discussion with others, but there was no sign of him. Professor Noteworthy sat nearby, busy making notes.

"Excuse me, Professor Noteworthy, but could you please tell us where we may find Professor Inabaox?" Snowball asked.

"Why, hello there young *kitdents*, I think he had an important meeting to attend," said Professor Noteworthy -- in his usual, nasal, singsong manner, and one note on his body rippled to the next level.

I think that note went from a C to a D, thought Goldie -- not entirely sure.

Then they remembered what Professor Inabaox had told them before the Defence Arts session. He had gone to meet Professor Quemarke for an important discussion.

Maybe he is still there, thought Snowball.

They thanked Professor Noteworthy and made their way to the principal's office. If their meeting finished early, it would give them a chance to convince Professor Inabaox today; otherwise, they would have to wait until the next day to meet him. They reached the principal's office but saw that they had shut the door, hence they sat on the bench outside to wait for Professor Inabaox to emerge. Muffled voices emanated from the room within, not clear enough to distinguish what they were saying. They waited there for a long time, whispering amongst themselves about what they would say to their professors in the most diplomatic way possible. Since school had ended for the day, kittens started lining up for their buses. All the directing-wasps also looked tired and were eager to go home. They stored the sign-boards in the storage room and huddled together for a last conversation with their friends. After nearly twenty minutes more, the door to the office opened. Still conversing, Professor Inabaox and Professor Quemarke stepped out of the room, only to stop short when they saw the waiting kittens.

"Hello everyone. Were you waiting to meet me?" Professor Inabaox greeted them cheerily, his large blue eyes focussed on them.

"Yes, sir," they said together hesitantly. They felt the principal's strict eyes upon them and suddenly became reticent.

"These are a few of the fifth-grade *kitdents*--who accompanied me on the search operation yesterday," said Professor Inabaox to Professor Quemarke.

"Good. I am proud of your courage at such a young age," said Professor Quemarke, and shook hands with each of them. He hesitated when he saw the bandage on Goldie's chin.

"Is this the result of battling our enemies yesterday?" he asked Goldie, raising his lynx-like eyebrows.

Professor Inabaox hurriedly interjected, "No sir, this results from an internal fight at school. Except for Kattie, no one else got injured during the search operation yesterday and even she is perfectly fine now."

"Internal fight? Let us use all our energies only to fight external forces that threaten our existence, unless there is a good reason," Professor Quemarke continued looking at Goldie--who nodded. "Why don't you come inside and tell us what you wanted to discuss?" he led the way into his office and shut the door behind them.

* * *

Joybob sat down on a boulder--under a bush, panting to catch his breath. Trixy joined him in a few minutes and sat down next to him, panting too. The sun was close to the western horizon, but they had made no headway today. They had tried to find an opening into the compound, in vain. Even the burrow they had painstakingly dug to remove the Core Fulcrum now looked sealed with cement. The burrow had taken them ten days to dig. Now they did not have that much time to dig a new one. They needed a quick solution.

"What do you hope to find there, anyway? The Core Fulcrum is with us. They are not foolish enough to keep information regarding the Pivot anywhere nearby. We will have to think of something else. I followed many robotic felids here and eavesdropped on their conversations but none of them talked about the Pivot," said Trixy. "It was so easy the last time. They were all so complacent. Now they all seem to be tight-lipped. No one talks loudly. They whisper incoherently and I cannot decipher what they discuss since I can't go too near them," he continued.

"Information about the Pivot may be available only with the most important felids. Let us go back to Lussian Peak -- to President Skailimet's office. I am sure he will reveal its location," said Joybob.

"How will we reach there? We are far away from Lussian Peak. I just don't have the energy to run that far."

"Are you crazy to think I will suggest running there? Silly, we will use the same method as the last time, we will hitch a ride."

"Not a bad idea," said Trixy, his cloak flapping behind him, as they both bounded towards the tarmac. Now all they had to do was wait for the eagle-shaped plane and hop onto it.

They sat around the settee in Professor Quemarke's office. The *kitdents* sat on one side facing the two professors sitting opposite them awkwardly. The professors patiently waited for them to begin.

"So, who will start?" Professor Inabaox asked finally.

"Sir, I will start," said Goldie. "I would like to request you to take us back to Trapesky on another search operation."

"Why do you want to go there again?" asked Professor Inabaox. He looked wary and uncomfortable.

"I believe the Core Fulcrum is there. I saw a few unusual lights there and believe those lights were a signal from it," said Goldie, shifting in his seat.

"Lights -- which only you saw. Remember? All of us were there, but no one saw them. It could have been anything. The sun was high up, and those glass bubbles were very refractive. You could have imagined it. In addition, we had scanned the entire area but had found nothing."

"There is a secret entrance in the well. I saw all the guards emanating from it, even though we found no door when we investigated it. We must have missed something."

"Maybe you are right about secret entrance in the well but I saw no other signs. No flattened grass, no sign of glistening dust and no other signs. It is too dangerous to go back there on a hunch."

"I have read about the Core Fulcrum's distress signal, but I always assumed it was folklore, since no one has reported seeing it yet. It doesn't stop with just one occurrence though," said Professor Quemarke.

"No one has seen it because no one has ever stolen it before, and maybe there was only one occurrence because later the enemies shrouded it in some opaque container. Hence, it could not send any more signals," insisted Goldie.

"Please -- Professor Quemarke and Professor Inabaox, we think Goldie is right. Please let us search in Trapesky again," pleaded Tufty. Snowball agreed and joined in.

"We attended Defence Arts training classes today and are better prepared to face our enemies," said Snowball.

"The enemies you deal with are very dangerous. They will kill to protect themselves and their territory against trespassers," said the principal. "We have a slot for a custom search operation after two weeks. I can ask them to include you all for that one and take you once more to Trapesky."

"Two weeks is a long time to wait. We don't have that much time," said Goldie, trying to build a case for urgency. "We should depart tomorrow."

"That is not possible," said Professor Inabaox. "I have already booked all the search slots to other counties for the next two weeks. Another trip to Trapesky will possible only after those."

No matter how long they debated, the decision of the adults was final. Another search operation would leave for Trapesky after two weeks. No sooner than that.

Goldie, Snowball and Tufty milled out of the office partially disappointed just before the buses left for the day. They ran to the school's parking ground, just as their mouse bus was about to depart. They met Kattie -- already seated in the alligator bus, informed her about the discussion and about the venue of the next Secrets training session, later in the night. They planned to meet in the Tunnel Garden beside Purrhy Lake at eight p.m., after dinner. By then, there would be no other kittens or cats around, and they could complete the session in peace.

Hisky saw Goldie and Snowball boarding their school bus in the last minute and realized they were planning something again. He thought of calling Salmonair, Ruffsaw and Kuting to his house later that night. They would reach the Manzar twins' house and spy on them to see what they were up-to. This time, he would have more company and support to fight them if required.

The night, Goldie and Snowball quickly finished dinner, much to the amazement of their mother -- Niamy. She was glad they had enjoyed the mackerel sandwiches. They ran upstairs and bolted the door of their room from inside. Goldie took a rope out of his cupboard that they usually used for camping trips and tied it to the study table's leg. Then he took his bag with the book in it and slung it over his back. Holding the rope, they jumped over the edge of the window, slowly climbed down, and dropped silently to the ground. As they passed the bay window of the drawing room, they noticed their parents watching the news about the missing Core Fulcrum on television. Luckily, their parents had their backs to the window and did not notice them. They ran to the gate, opened it, ran outside and silently shut the gate behind them. They did not realize they were being watched from the bushes across the road.

The Tunnel Garden officially closed at seven p.m. but the walls were not very high. With one jump, they were inside the compound. Kattie was already waiting under the pavilion near the entrance.

"What took you so long?" she whispered. "I had to hitch a ride from an old farmer neighbour near my house. He drove his duck buggy into town to collect a few supplies. He said he will pick me up in an hour's time, so I am running against the clock."

"Mom was serving us dinner. Did not want to leave before we finished at the usual time," said Snowball.

"Did not want to arouse any suspicion," said Goldie.

Soon they saw Tufty outside the garden -- who waved goodbye to his elder brother -- Pufty. His brother also had a tuft on his head. It was their family's key physical feature.

"What did you tell your brother? You know this is confidential," said Snowball.

"I told him I needed your help for an urgent project submission. My brother is going to his friend's house for a sleepover, so he will pick me up only tomorrow morning."

Great, now the three of them had to climb into the bedroom without being noticed.

"Come on, let's get started," said Kattie. "As explained earlier, I don't have all night like the three of you."

The tunnel-garden featured tunnels of all shapes and sizes. Goldie and Snowball had grown up playing in this garden and knew it like the backs of their paws. There was an interesting maze in the centre of the garden that they were masters of, but it had taken many weeks of going around in circles before they had become experts. To the untrained mind, the maze was a tough and convoluted challenge.

Ruffsaw and Salmonair wait outside the Tunnel Garden

"Follow me!" said Goldie as he darted inside the main tunnel. They all followed him. The walls were lit by glow worms that worked there during the night shift. They slept in transparent cases hung on the wall and emitted a glow that threw shadows all around. "Please stick together. There are some tricky parts of this garden that only both Snowball and I know well."

They turned left, then right and then left again, till they arrived at a fork. Goldie then took the right tunnel to exit into a central garden. He immediately entered the maze, weaving through the rocky paths until he arrived at a small trapdoor. There he bent, lifted the door and admitted everyone before following them inside. Once all of them were inside the chamber, he pulled the trapdoor down. This chamber, too, was lit up by glow worms on the wall.

"This is one of the many chambers inside the maze we used to play in. It is almost impossible to find unless you know the maze well. Even though this place is dimly lit, we should be able to see the images inside the orb. Let's begin," said Goldie, removing the book from the bag.

Outside the Tunnel Garden, Hisky, Salmonair, Ruffsaw and Kuting discussed what to do next. Ruffsaw and Salmonair were not sure about entering the tunnels. They thought it was better to wait outside and keep watch. Hisky and Kuting jumped over the wall to enter the main tunnel. The big tunnel turned left and right for a distance of approximately four-hundred metres, finally ending at a fork. Kuting took the left turn in the fork and Hisky took the right one. Soon Hisky exited into a beautiful, fragrant garden. In the centre of this garden, he could see a large rocky structure, with an entrance to a tunnel inside it. He knew Goldie and his gang had gone there.

Inside the chamber, the orb sprung to life when the next session started. The images played scenes from ancient times when King Skatzer was in exile. All his citizens practised the techniques taught by Dr. Diadoms. The Core Fulcrum stood on top of a tall pedestal in a glass casing in the centre of the town to energize everyone with its magical rays of light. They grew stronger day by day, performing tasks that were hitherto impossible.

"The Core Fulcrum works best when placed under the open sky, when you expose it to the light from the sun," said Dr. Diadoms.

So, maybe the Core Fulcrum was being forced into an enclosed space when I saw the signal, thought Goldie.

"Today I shall teach you how to make objects float in the air--just like a hovercraft using the power of the Core Fulcrum. Unfortunately, since the Core Fulcrum is not in front of you, try this trick at the next available opportunity when it is. Graphene aerogel is the lightest substance created in the world so far. Though we had created a similar substance during prehistoric times, the current invention is much lighter than that. It is so light that you can place it on top of a duckling's back without its realisation. It will stay suspended on top of the feathery wisps, without touching its skin. It weighs just '0.16' grams per cubic centimetre and is seven times lighter than air. To make an object float, you need to coat it with Graphene aerogel and then run the Core Fulcrum or its ore extract over the coated object. Sometimes its ore dust will do the trick, once sprinkled over the coated object."

The moving images in front changed to show them felids coating objects in workshops using the lightest substance. They sprinkled some magical dust over it and viola; the objects started floating. They created vehicles out of these new objects that allowed them to hover around magically.

This is a revelation, but how will we get our hold of Graphene aerogel, thought Snowball. *The substance must be available in the science lab. I must explore the lab next time. How else did we make those floating ghosts work during science class?*

They asked a few more questions to Dr. Diadoms to clarify their doubts, which he patiently answered. It relieved them that the session was over quickly -- with no interruptions -- when he suddenly started looking worried.

"I must go now, while you deal with the intruder. Anyway, I have completed the lesson for the day. Goodbye until the next time and all the best with creating floating objects," he said and disappeared.

Oh, no, not again, thought Goldie. *When will we have peace?*

"Exit rainbow rondure," said Kattie this time, and they dropped to the floor of the chamber.

At that very instant, they heard a loud scream from the maze near them.

"HELP! SOMEONE PLEASE HELP ME. I am lost in this maze," the voice said.

"That sounds like Hisky," said Snowball, swishing his grey tail around with growing irritation. "He just can't seem to leave us alone!"

"PLEASE HELP ME TOO. I am thoroughly lost," called out another voice.

"Now that sounds like Kuting," said Tufty.

"Should we help them or leave them alone?" asked Kattie.

"I have another idea," said Goldie, as he whispered a plan in their ears. They thought it was a wonderful plan.

They left the two screaming kittens in the maze and jumped out of the back gate. From outside, although faint, they could still hear Hisky's and Kuting's screams. A passing vehicle could discern the noise if they listened intently. Kattie's neighbour had reached the outskirts of the garden, so she waved goodbye and departed with him. Goldie, Snowball and Tufty made their way back into the house and climbed up the rope into the room. Niamy and Paka were still in the drawing room watching weather news on TV. Once in the room, Snowball and Goldie unbolted their room door to go downstairs.

"Dad, Mom, I think I hear someone in distress at the Tunnel Garden," said Goldie.

"What distress?" Paka asked, turning the volume of the TV down.

"Someone is calling out for help," said Snowball.

"I hear nothing--" said Niamy, surprised at the news.

"You hear nothing because the TV is on, and its drowning out the cries. We could hear it loudly from our veranda," said Goldie.

Deciding to investigate, Paka and Niamy switched off the TV and walked down the hillock to the Tunnel Garden. They saw Salmonair and Ruffsaw outside the gate, looking inside with a worried expression, debating about what to do next. Then the parents heard the cries.

"HELP! Salmonair, Ruffsaw, could you please save me?" a voice pleaded.

"PLEASE HELP ME. I AM GOING AROUND IN CIRCLES FOR SO LONG HERE," another voice screamed.

"Hi there, do you know if someone needs help?" Paka asked the two seniors, who literally jumped out of their skins when they saw him.

"Y-yes. One of our j-juniors got lost inside somewhere," said Salmonair.

"We don't know the maze well enough to help them," said Ruffsaw, equally jittered.

"Let us see. You please wait here. We will rescue them," said Niamy.

Both Paka and Niamy bounded into the garden to locate the lost kittens. They returned soon with Hisky and Kuting in tow.

"What are all of you doing here after normal hours? This garden shuts at seven p.m. and now it is past bedtime." said Paka, looking at each kitten.

"We-we arrived here in the evening but lost our way inside the maze," lied Hisky.

"Yes, we lost our way in the maze," seconded Kuting.

"That is strange. Usually, there is a caretaker - who searches the whole garden before he shuts the gates. Seems like you did not respond when he was checking," said Niamy, distrusting them.

Goldie, Snowball and Tufty peered out of the veranda near their room to observe the scene below. They could see the stalkers deep in conversation with the adults. They giggled and performed high-fives.

"Which school do you study in?" Paka asked the dreaded question.

"Meow Wow High School sir," said Salmonair, feeling responsible for the debacle.

"I know the principal of Meow Wow High. I will talk to him tomorrow about this. You may go home now," he chastised them sternly.

The four kittens gulped and ran away from the Tunnel Garden as fast as they could, much to the merriment of the observers from the veranda.

* * *

CHAPTER FIFTEEN

Kindness and Kitdart

Tufty left Goldie and Snowball's house in the morning through the window, before their parents woke up. The next day when they reached school, the entire building's configuration had completely changed again. Goldie saw a big hornet holding directions instead of the usual wasp that buzzed in that corner.

"Hello, there hornet," said Goldie, noting the directions to his classroom. "Where is the wasp today?"

"He is on sick leave. I am his cousin from the back-yard. Today I am on double duty," said the hornet.

"Would you know why the school keeps changing its structure so much every day? Why couldn't they have constructed fixed buildings that never changed?" asked Snowball. He always wanted to know the answer to that.

"The management council of the school says it's for security reasons. Only felids like you can understand the signs we hold," it said.

For security reasons? Now why would they need security? Food for thought, thought Goldie as he bounded towards the moving elevators.

Trixy and Joybob struggled against the steel bars. No matter how much they tried to chew their way out, it did not work. Trixy's mind drifted to the situation that had brought them here. They were waiting on the tarmac under a parked vehicle for a long time -- long enough for the sun to descend to the west. Finally, they saw the eagle plane. All the passengers got into the plane, but there was no sign of President Skailimet. The last to board the plane was the pilot. That was their cue. They rushed towards the open door of the luggage compartment. However, as soon as they climbed the ladder to the compartment, a net descended around them both. A felid held the net with a handle and twisted it securely.

"Gotcha!" he said triumphantly, placing them both in a steel cage and locking it. Then, he kept the steel cage in the luggage compartment along with several other cartons, where they stayed until they reached Lussian Peak. After that, the crew transported them to a pharmaceutical laboratory where they stacked the cage in the basement with several other caged animals.

"So much for being an intelligent spy. I don't want to become a nameless experiment," said Joybob, trying hard to chew through the cage again.

"It is all your fault. It was your idea to go to Lussian Peak again," said Trixy. Acquisition of the Pivot started feeling like a fuzzy, distant dream to him.

Joybob felt in his pocket, where he had stored a pinch of the star dust left behind by the Core Fulcrum. Maybe, just maybe, they had a sliver of a chance.

Professor Quemarke in his office

Professor Quemarke sat in his office, staring at the pastel-cream slates on the wall behind his desk. Many of them displayed ever changing portraits; others displayed moving images. Most of those showed a much younger version of himself, holding trophies and wearing medals. Out of all the portraits displayed, there was one that was his favourite. In that, he was being crowned as a Goldermew by the President of Mew Scape, President Mace. They considered it an honour that was the most difficult to earn -- sometimes it took twenty long years, and even after that time, most of them did not achieve this honour. He had completed it in eight years -- a feat hitherto unheard of. There were only twenty-one Goldermews in the whole of Eartavista. These Goldermews had reached the pinnacle in the proprietary art of Orenda and Defence -- a tradition that had continued through ancient times. To become a Goldermew, they had to become experts in all aspects of the art: mentally, physically and spiritually. They had to be knowledgeable, skilled, fearless, empathetic and patriotic. Sometimes, they had to make difficult decisions to choose the good of the citizens over their own family, which was the hardest aspect.

Another portrait that was his second favourite was the one that showed him being promoted to the guardian of the Core Fulcrum. It was the highest honour in Eartavista, shared by only two people: President Skailimet, the president of Lussian Peak and he. This honour was a privilege bestowed on him by the citizens. It was a unanimous vote of credibility. They voted a new guardian into power, only after the previous one retired -- which was usually on their death-bed. He had become the guardian when President Mace had died. Only two guardians existed in the world -- usually. However, because of the circumstances, and the disappearance of the divine cube, both President Skailimet and he had voted to promote Professor Inabaox to a discretionary title of Vice Guardian -- the only such discretionary title in Eartavista.

The news of the disappearance of the Core Fulcrum had spread like wildfire, because of which their credibility was at stake. They had to find it sooner than later. Professor Inabaox was also a Goldermew, one who everyone trusted implicitly -- whose credibility was of the highest standards. Now, they had entrusted him with the quest to find the Core Fulcrum for the whole of Eartavista. Once he found it, he would move it to its new hideout, for which they had already completed the construction.

How could the Core Fulcrum have disappeared? There was security all around the compound. Not only that, sophisticated alarm and camera systems monitored it all day and night. Slates captured moving images and vignettes from all angles, and infrared heat sensors scanned for invisible invaders on the ground. Those images got relayed to surveillance centres around the world. None of the images revealed anything much. One slate had captured a moving image of the Core Fulcrum dive into a hole under itself that had materialised out of nowhere. That was initially inexplicable. On further investigation by Professor Inabaox, they had found a long burrow under the site, leading to a tree far away from the compound. The tree was beside the tarmac they used for flying planes and gliders. There was no sign of anyone else by the time they discovered the burrow. The enemy was very intelligent.

A knock on the door interrupted his thoughts. There were five cats and four *kitdents* outside. Yes, he had summoned them after a conversation last night with Mr. Paka. They were: Hisky and his father, Kuting and his mother, Salmonair and his father, Ruffsaw and his uncle and Professor Inabaox. When they all assembled in the room, they shut the door behind themselves. Professor Inabaox began by addressing the four *kitdents* in the room.

"As you all know, a distinguished citizen reported that four of you were loitering around the main Tunnel Garden late last night. Though it is usually not the business of the school management to get involved in any incidents outside its school premises, we have called you for questioning today. The only reason for that is that all four of you are members of the Curiosity Kills the Cat club. Two of you -- Hisky and Kuting got lost in the maze and started screaming for help. Is that right? If so, this can be of serious consequence to us -- especially if it is in connection to class activities. So, to clear the air, we would like to ask you, what were your intentions of going to the Tunnel Garden together?"

Hisky looked very uncomfortable as he bent his head down. Kuting looked around awkwardly, not knowing how to start. Salmonair and Ruffsaw also hung their heads down -- tongue-tied. Before anyone could say anything, Hisky's father spoke.

"I am sure he had a good reason, or maybe he just wanted to play. You mentioned this garden is outside the school premises. Why don't you leave them alone? Did you pull me out of office to attend this inane meeting? Just to ask what my son was doing in a Tunnel Garden at night?"

"Sir, out of due respect, would you rather we'd left him in the maze screaming for help?" Professor Quemarke said. "He could have been there till next morning until the caretaker opened the garden to the public. Would that have been fine? Think of how that would have affected you? Be thankful that someone was nearby to rescue them. We only want to inform you for your kitten's safety and benefit."

When he heard that, Hisky's father turned to Hisky and pointed his index toe at him.

"You told me you were going to your friend -- Kuting's house. He lives at least five kilometres from the place they found you. I don't want to be embarrassed ever like this again -- do you hear me?"

Hisky nodded his head silently.

"I will cut all your pocket mice if I get a whiff of anything like this," Hisky's father turned to the principal again. "I am very sorry this happened and assure you on his behalf that he will not repeat this behaviour."

Kuting's mother too promptly apologised profusely to the principal, mentioning it would not happen again. Salmonair's father and Ruffsaw's uncle also looked quite displeased about the situation and apologised. They all left the office after a few minutes, looking thoroughly embarrassed. Goldie, Snowball, Clawcia and Billy passed by as Hisky, Kuting, Salmonair and Ruffsaw exited the office. Hisky glared at the twins, knowing that somehow, the rambunctious duo had a part to play in this.

Professor Neko waited for everyone to sit down before beginning her session on kindness as a way of life. She showed the class two clay pots with exactly the same variety and colour of rose plants in each. One flower drooped while the other happily bloomed.

"This is a simple example to show you how kindness makes a difference. Here you see two similar plants in two different pots. One droops sadly while the other one blooms happily. The gardener grafted both saplings from the same parent plant. One of them was not getting enough sun, but the gardener did not notice it in the corner, and it started drooping. I am sure, with enough attention and sunlight, this too will recover," she said, taking the plant to the window under the sun. She put a cup of water in the pot and sprinkled some sparkling dust on the plant. It slowly sprung up until it faced the sun. She went back to the front desk and showed it to the *kitdents*. Amazement writ all over their faces, they clapped. Many of them were fond of gardening, especially to grow varieties of grass.

"An invisible, magical force called Orenda pervades each natural object (both living and non-living). It is up to us to recognise this power. Kindness helps us to recognise and connect with it. When you are kind, your mind opens, and an open mind exudes positive energy. When you touch someone's life with that positive energy, it gets paid forward, and the reaction continues like a ripple until it encircles the universe. Could you please give me examples of when kindness can make a difference in someone's life?"

Katzchen raised his paw and said,

"Ma'am, when we help the blind or the elderly to cross the road."

"Good."

"When we help our parents at home and in the kitchen," said Billy.

"I was about to say the same thing. The day I help them, the food is tastier," said Clawcia.

Everyone giggled but agreed with her.

"Yes."

"When we help our younger siblings with their homework," said Kattie.

"Correct."

"When we fight for our world and protect its citizens," said Goldie.

"That would define courage over kindness; although courage is a greater version of kindness. Good."

"When we take revenge against any wrongdoing," said Hisky, glaring at Goldie.

"Revenge? No. No. Kindness never thinks about revenge," said Professor Neko, swishing her tail around alarmedly. Her eyes looked wider and bluer than usual.

"When we help a friend in need," said Snowball, glaring at Hisky.

"Yes, that is more like it."

The examples continued for ten minutes more. After that exercise, Professor Neko wrote a few principles for them to follow for a life of kindness. She provided several examples for each principle.

After Professor Neko's session, the *kitdents* of grade five dashed to the rear of the school building for the next Kitdart training session. There would practise the Climb section in greater detail to make sure everyone got the technique right. They assembled in the indoor stadium before Coach Dudgeble walked in -- dribbling himself on the floor. He had folded his legs up, but his left front paw kept tapping his head so he bounced up and down like a basketball.

"Good morning, *kitdents*. Today we shall practise the Climb section of Kitdart to understand its intricacies. Please divide yourselves into six teams of three each, as we have six racing tracks. Since there are eighteen in this class, you can form exactly six teams," he said.

Hisky, Mewtiony and Gattino formed the first team and stood behind the starting line of the first track. Goldie, Snowball and Billy formed the second team, Kattie, Tufty and Clawcia formed the third team, Katzchen, Hirra and Yavru formed the fourth team, Melowflues, Misty and Grimis formed the fifth team, and Mao, Pompom and Cica formed the sixth team. They all put on their safety harnesses.

"Even though you have tried this race before, let me remind you of the rules. Climbing a fixed rope successfully gives you five points, climbing a floating rope gives you ten. If you touch any part of your body on the ground,

A kitten climbs the snake rope

you lose five points and if you fall, you lose ten. If all your legs touch the ground, we treat it as a fall, no matter how gracefully you do it. There are no live animals in this race; all vegetables, snakes, and worms are fake, made of paper or jelly. Do not panic like the last time."

Hisky, Goldie, Kattie, Katzchen, Melowflues, and Mao were to in line to start the race. As soon as they would reach the finish line on top of the platform, Mr. Dudgeble would blow the whistle again, signalling the second set of teammates to start the climb, followed by the third set. Coach Dudgeble pressed a switch on the wall, following which the ropes descended, making a hissing sound. The track had twenty ropes, ten of them fixed and the other ten--floating. Floating ropes kept moving up and down at varying speeds. The rapidly moving ones were the most challenging.

Mao wondered whether she could climb the rapidly moving ones without falling to the ground.

At the start of the whistle, they set off. They launched themselves on the first rope--a fixed one. Goldie soon jumped onto the next rope--a slow-moving one. Hisky, Kattie and the others followed suit on their respective tracks. Since the third rope was the fixed kind, it was a cake-walk. The fourth one--made of plastic--although fixed, was smooth and slippery, since it had an oily coating. Goldie grabbed it but started slipping towards the ground rapidly. Just as he almost reached the ground, he jumped onto the next rope that had a jelly-like surface and was moving upwards. Phew! It had been a close call. Hisky was not so lucky and slid rapidly downwards. He landed with all four paws on the ground. Kattie also slid but touched only one paw on the ground before jumping onto the next. Mao, Katzchen and Melowflues also fell to the ground because of that slippery rope. Goldie led the score-board so far.

He dug his claws into the jelly-like rope but it started cracking. He left it and jumped onto the sixth rope that was moving downwards. This rope was made of a green, gooey substance. *Yuck!* He left it as soon as he could to jump onto the seventh rope -- a fixed one made of coconut coir.

This was prickly, but much safer, he thought. He waited a second to get his breath back, which was a mistake because Hisky, Kattie and the others were hot on his heels. He jumped onto the eighth rope, which was a fixed one made of catnip. It smelled so good that he wanted to eat it. However, bringing his focus back to the game, he jumped onto the ninth one -- made of cotton, which was moving so rapidly that his tail touched the ground before he could jump onto the tenth one -- a fixed one that looked exactly like a snake with scales, but was artificial. The snake turned towards him baring its fangs and menacingly flicked its tongue at him. Focusing on the job at hand, he ignored the snake and jumped onto the next one. He quickly covered the fixed eleventh and twelfth ones without a problem, despite their thorny surfaces. By now, he was high above the ground. He saw Hisky and Kattie catching up with him on the neighbouring tracks. The next four floating ropes were moving so rapidly that he had to calculate his jumps with precision. He jumped onto the first one made of clay, just in time to see the next three aligned in the centre above the ground. Those ropes, made with cactus leaves, cardboard and chalk respectively, drifted upwards. Treating it like a sprinting track, he bounded across the three of them to reach the seventeenth rope, made of flimsy tissue paper. It tore under his weight, making him fall. His rear paw touched the floor before he grabbed the next floating rope, covered with jam. The jam started sticking to his paws. Ignoring the urge to lick his paws, he clutched the next fixed one made of shiny and slippery fish scales. He held onto the rope with his claws and climbed higher using the gaps between the scales. The final rope was a floating one covered with red ants. As he jumped onto it, they immediately started crawling all over his body. Realising these were not real; he held onto the rope, which was going upwards and landed on the platform safely. As soon as he landed, he dusted off the ants. It was creepy! He rejoiced as he was the first to finish the race. Hisky landed on the platform soon after he did, followed by Kattie. They too danced around as they dusted themselves. Katzchen, Mao and Melowflues took longer to complete the race. Coach Dudgeble blew the whistle for the second set of races to begin. Snowball won that race. The coach blew the whistle for the third and final set. He adjudged Grimis and Cica as the tied winners for that race. All of them danced agitatedly to dust off the critters they had collected. Gattino, as usual, had the lowest score. Sports did not interest him at all.

After all races were over, the coach calculated the final total. Goldie's team won with the highest score of five-hundred-and-thirty points, followed by Kattie's team with four-hundred-and-sixty points. Hisky's team was third with three-hundred-and-ninety points. Goldie, Snowball and Billy were glad to have won. They formed a huddle and hopped around together.

"Yay, we won!" they said happily.

Coach Dudgeble walked over to congratulate the winners, looking thrilled with the overall performance of the *kitdents*. He was hoping the best player of Kitdart would be from this batch. Hisky's team was not happy, as expected. Hisky realised it was best to stop stalking them around and instead focus on Kitdart.

That day, Goldie, Snowball, Tufty and Kattie skipped the Secrets' training session since they were all feeling tired.

* * *

CHAPTER SIXTEEN

A Disturbing Encounter

That night, Goldie could not sleep for a long time. He tossed and turned around in his hanging basket. Contrary to his situation, Snowball lay fast asleep in the next basket. He felt guilty about missing Dr. Diadoms' training session and worried about their mission. With increased delay, the enemies would get closer to the Pivot. He would never forgive himself if that happened. After almost midnight, he fell asleep slowly.

Suddenly, he opened his eyes when he felt someone else in the room and felt his hackles rise. Sitting upright with alacrity, he realised he was not in his room at all, but in the middle of sand dunes far away from home. He sat on a large velvet seat, which moved forward rapidly -- being carried ahead by unknown creatures. They reached a big tract of enormous cacti and stopped. There they saw cobbled paths all around these large plants, and on a closer look, each of these cacti were homes. With curtain adorned windows and doors carved into their sides, these cacti housed mole-rat bandicoots. Little balconies decorated the front of windows that opened over the cobbled paths. The mole-rats scurried around in their homes, oblivious to the stranger outside. It was a miniature township for the affluent. The unseen bearers took him to the largest cactus plant in the centre of the exurb and laid him down. Four mole-rat bandicoots stood beside the velvet platform, waiting for someone to arrive. A massive door opened from the cactus in the front, and a large, grisly mole-rat bandicoot stepped out. He looked like their king, since he wore a crown and had a red-coloured, flowing cloak around his shoulders. A scar ran down his right cheek, and a stitched tuft of brown fur blocked out his right eye. He held a black stone in his left front paw, which gleamed dangerously at Goldie. As soon as Goldie stood up, he felt himself getting sucked into the stone. His skin, fur, flesh and bones started turning into dust and merging into the black stone.

"Welcome to the destruction of you and your kind! We have the pivot and we will not spare you," the king said and started cackling loudly. The remaining mole-rats also joined in.

"Stop!" said Goldie, trying to run back to the seat in vain. It was too late. The entire world started spinning around him until it became a blur.

A paw grabbed him through the blur and tried to pull him up, but he resisted. He did not want to listen to these rats.

"Leave me alone, you -- mole-rat. Stop grabbing my fur," he said, spinning round and round rapidly.

The paw tugged at his fur harder.

"Goldie! Goldie!" a familiar voice said through the swirling blur around him.

Goldie opened his eyes reluctantly to see Snowball's face inches away from his. He was back in his room, in his basket, and the mole-rats had vanished.

"Goldie! Were you having a nightmare?" Snowball asked him. "I saw you tossing around and shouting in your basket -- that is why I woke you up. Are you all right?"

That is when Goldie realized he had been dreaming. He nodded his head at Snowball.

"Yes, I am fine. I dreamed mole-rats kidnapped me and took me to their king. The king had the Pivot and tried to destroy me with it. It was a horrible feeling."

"Oops. Yes, I heard you calling me a mole-rat several times." Snowball chuckled.

"This dream convinces me even more that the Core Fulcrum is with the mole-rats at Trapesky. As we had flown away from there, I had seen the king in the veranda, shaking his fist at us. He looked exactly like the ugly mole-rat in my nightmare. The universe is sending me a signal. We have to go back there -- Snowball, we just have to," said Goldie.

"Look, you know I am already convinced and besides, would do anything for you, believe me." Snowball sat next to Goldie.

Goldie tapped his brother's tail with his own.

"I would do the same. That is what brothers are for," said Goldie, glad about having a brother like Snowball. It made the world a better place.

Clemawp - the laboratory cleaner walked into the basement to check on the animals. He needed to clean up all the cages before all the technicians arrived at Lussian Peak Prime Laboratory. He began working. It was almost an hour before he cleaned up all the old cages. Then he turned his attention to the new ones delivered the previous evening. He almost finished cleaning all of them when he saw something strange under a new cage. He went back to inspect. The cage had two mole-rat bandicoots in it, but under the cage, he saw a peculiar, glistening patch. Strange, iridescent rays of light emanated from the patch. Doing a double take, he retrieved the rag once more to clean it.

"Chemicals, they are so careless with chemicals, but I have to do all the cleaning up. If anything happens to the animals, I get blamed," he muttered, lifting the cage up to clean the strange patch. He cleaned up the patch with the rag, then dropped the rag along with the cleaning mop in the bucket filled with dirty, soapy water. The water also contained other cleaning agents for a better result. After cleaning the remaining cages, he proceeded to the basin to wash his paws. He usually looked forward to a cup of coffee in the cafeteria upstairs before ending his morning shift. His friend Mewmaid usually accompanied him. He hummed his favourite tune, swaying to an invisible beat. "Oh, I went to Calabamba with my tango on my knee. Hum, hum, hum, hum, hum, hum, hum, hum, hum, hum, hum, hum, hum, hum, hum, hum," he doled out, imagining himself singing on a big stage. He aspired to be a world-famous

Clemawp gets scared of the ghost

singer one day. Wiping his paws on the towel next to the basin, he turned around to witness a hair-raising sight.

The rag and the mop had risen into the air in such a manner that the overall effect looked like a hooded creature atop a post. The post floated above the bucket and swayed from side-to-side. The dark, deep, and hollow folds of the floating rag looked like the face of a dangerous ghost, an augury of death. Delicate wisps-of-light emanated below the hood, with a trail rising from the bucket.

"G-g-ghost! G-g-ghost!" screamed Clemawp, gulping while gripping the wash basin behind him for dear life.

The hooded creature rose higher and moved towards him. That was all the encouragement that Clemawp needed. He bolted out of the door as fast as possible to report the matter to the security staff.

"Aargh! Leave me alone!" he said, as he dashed up the staircase, leaving the door wide open behind him.

By the time he came back with the security guards, the 'ghost' had already moved into the corridor. They all took one look at the hooded creature and bolted away upstairs in fear, shutting all the doors to the basement. They felt they had safely locked up the spirit. The lead security guard resolved to talk to the head technician -- Mr. Microscap about it, and if required, report the matter to the police.

"Today, I shall take you to the Catyons," said Professor Piquant, as the *kitdents* assembled in the clearing behind the school -- in front of the musical fountains. "There, we will pick some squishy Orangellos. Orangellos are the half-formed eggs of the Orangeros -- some of the largest birds in Eartavista. They are three times larger than us and can attack us if they notice us. When the eggs are perfect, they have a hard shell; however, when their eggs form imperfectly, their shells become very squishy. Those eggs will never hatch and are a delicacy. Today we shall pick at least five Orangellos and make omelettes out of them. There is a huge colony of the birds near the Catyons, so I am sure we will be successful with our hunting expedition."

Hawk gliders waited nearby as the *kitdents* got into them -- four at a time. The hornet guided them towards the waiting vehicles. Apparently, his cousin was still unwell. After they sat safely within the hawks, Professor Piquant boarded the first one and shouted so that everyone could hear her voice over the flapping of the wings.

"Today we will fly high over the Catyons. These birds like to nest on ledges on top of very high cliffs. Keep your eyes open for very large orange-coloured birds. In case you see a bird approach you, lie down flat and stay still. It gets confused with stationary objects and invariably leaves them alone. Quickly approach its nest and check for the hardness and translucency of the eggs. Drop the Orangellos into the baskets provided, but leave the white ones alone. It will chase and peck us if we take those."

Misty looked uncomfortable and asked, "Ma'am, are we going to the Ghastly Catyons? Is it the place where the ghosts live?"

Professor Piquant burst out laughing.

"No dear, these are not the Ghastly Catyons. Those Catyons are much farther north from these ordinary ones. You don't have to worry about encountering ghosts."

Misty looked relieved.

The five hawks took off in the air with a flurry of flapping wings. The kittens watched with absolute glee as they left the school buildings behind to soar high above the clouds. This was the highest that Goldie and Snowball had ever flown. The dragonfly bus could only fly at the height of treetops, but this vehicle was a king of the skies. The hawks took advantage of the wind current and straightened their wings to sail smoothly ahead.

Within minutes they reached their destination, a place between Mew Scape and Furrybank. The Catyons loomed in the front -- a pastel green and peach-coloured landscape filled with peaks and troughs because of the ancient canyons -- created by the Mawina river that flowed through it. Mawina also flowed through the neighbouring Furrybank county -- the largest port in Eartavista. All the sailing competitions during Catalympics were held on this river at Furrybank.

Professor Piquant saw a viewing gallery ahead and asked the pilots to land nearby. This would offer them a good viewpoint to observe any nesting grounds. Once they stopped, she taught them how to spot the birds using their superior vision and to climb trees on which they built nests.

"It is very important to slink on the ground and be as immobile as possible. Climb the tree that contains the nest with very little vibration from your feet. Stealth is of utmost importance while hunting. It is also important to take advantage of the surrounding shrubbery to stay camouflaged."

They practised the silent, slinking and lunging movements until they mastered the technique. Then, they stepped in front of the viewing gallery to spot the birds. Soon Grimis spotted a large flock near a peak not very far from them. He boarded the hawk along with Cica, Melowflues and Katzchen and instructed the pilot to follow the Orangeros. Snowball, Goldie, Billy and Tufty--who sat in another one, followed his. Hisky, Gattino, Mewtiony and Yavru followed a fast-moving flock in the opposite direction. The others also spotted birds at different places and guided their hawks behind them. Professor Piquant told them to re-assemble at the viewing gallery in precisely thirty minutes even if they had collected no Orangellos.

The large flock that Grimis's hawk was following suddenly turned in another direction into the lazily gliding clouds. The hawks followed closely behind. As soon as the clouds cleared, they saw a huge colony of nests atop several leafless trees. There were three to four such nest-laden trees on every steep ledge. Grimis spotted a nest with an egg that looked darker than the rest and asked the pilot to swoop downwards. Goldie's hawk targeted another nest on the other side. They successfully landed their gliders on the ledges above the ones with the nests and climbed down. As soon as they reached the ledge of the nest, there was a shrill cry from one bird circling in the sky. It swooped down towards Goldie and Snowball -- its sharp orange beak ready to strike.

"Lie down! Lie down!" shouted Goldie, and the four of them slammed to the ground to lie down flat.

The huge bird swooped down and landed on its nest, surveying its four eggs -- one of which was an Orangello. The bird had a mustard yellow body with bright, orange-coloured wings. It had green eyes outlined in blue-and-yellow and a sharp, curved, orange-coloured beak. This was a bird of prey. After surveying its nest, it flew heavily to the ground and walked around suspiciously. As it walked around, its orange claws abutted Billy's face, making his heart jump into his throat. After five excruciating minutes, satisfied that nothing was threatening its eggs, the bird took off into the sky.

"Ah, my diaphragm moves again," said Billy, clutching his chest with his paws.

Goldie slunk up the tree slowly, stopping intermittently, to not distract the bird again. Snowball crept up the tree behind him. Tufty and Billy stayed on the ground with the basket. As slowly as he could, Goldie removed the Orangello from the nest, without upsetting the balance of the other eggs and handed it to Snowball. Snowball passed it to Tufty and Billy -- who placed it in the leafy basket and covered it. Then, as slowly as they could, they walked to the rear of the cliff to climb the ledge where their hawk lay waiting on standby.

After thirty minutes, everyone's gliders had reached the viewing gallery except Hisky's. The assembled *kitdents* had collected four Orangellos in total. Hirra was missing a small tuft of fur from his ear, where the bramble from the tree had poked him. No other *kitdent* appeared hurt after this assignment. Professor Piquant panicked when forty minutes passed with no sign of Hisky's hawk, and was thinking of going on a rescue mission, when they appeared from behind a tall peak on the northern side. Their glider flew towards them at almost hypersonic speed.

CHAPTER SEVENTEEN

Universal Action Controller

Hisky's hawk reached the viewing gallery site before the others could blink their eyes. They all looked pale. They handed over one Orangello to an anxious-looking Professor Piquant.

"What happened?" asked Professor Piquant. "Why were you so late and why was your hawk flying above the permissible speed limit? These gliders have to follow certain rules too, you know."

It was some time before they recovered, as they appeared shaken. Their paws shivered perceptibly.

"It-it's true. Th-they exist," said Hisky.

"Who they?" Misty wanted to know.

"Ghosts. Hundreds of them. Small, big, fat, thin, young, old and all kinds of them," said Gattino.

"They chased us," said Yavru.

"And one of them grabbed my leg," said Gattino

"It looked like a cross between a witch and a scarecrow," said Hisky.

Misty gasped and so did many others.

"Where did you all go?" Professor Piquant enquired with growing annoyance.

"Ghastly Catyons," said Mewtiony.

"I told you that the Ghastly Catyons are much farther to the north. I restricted this hunt to the Orange Catyons. Why did you fly so far up north?" Professor Piquant looked thoroughly displeased.

"Our hawk followed the Orangeros closely. They turned around and flew in a different direction. Before we realised it, they led us to the Ghastly Catyons."

"I am glad you returned unhurt. I can't say others have been so lucky. Let us return to school immediately now," said Professor Piquant not wanting to continue the discussion, with the worry of scaring the other *kitdents*.

They all boarded their hawks without another word and returned to school. Soon they were in the school kitchen, making omelettes. With each egg, they could make twenty omelettes. After completing the omelettes, they packed them in cartons made of leaves for dispatch to the cafeteria. Hisky and his gang still looked rattled as they left the kitchen.

"I wonder what they saw?" Snowball asked Goldie. "I don't mind going there on a picnic to see what it's like. Maybe we will run into Gattino's ghost there."

"You heard Professor Piquant. They were lucky they escaped unhurt. We should focus on retrieving the Core Fulcrum and leave these adventurous, but distracting jaunts for another time," said Goldie.

At Lussian Peak Prime Laboratory's main office, Microscap listened closely to what Clemawp and the two security guards recounted to him. It was a very interesting story, but one that he found hard to believe. He stood up to go to the basement where they claimed to have locked up the spirit. Opening the door to the basement, he walked downstairs to the corridor outside the storage area, followed hesitantly by the others. The soggy mop and rag lay on the floor in the middle of the corridor.

So much for a ghost story. These cats have led me on a wild goose chase. They should gossip less and work more. Gossip makes them daydream too much, he thought.

"Is this the ghost you saw?" he turned around and asked the three of them, who looked perplexed.

"Um... there was a spirit within the rag when I saw it. Now it seems to have left," said Clemawp, looking around in case the spirit was still around.

"Yes, he is right. We saw it too," said the guards, scanning the whole corridor in case it materialized.

"Hmm... What was the last thing you did before you saw the so-called ghost?" asked Mr. Microscap, getting exasperated with their dramatic antics.

"I cleaned up an unusual glittery stain under one cage. The stain was emitting strange rays of light. I cleaned it up, and then was washing my hands when the spirit appeared," said Clemawp.

Mr. Microscap's ears stood up when he heard that and asked Clemawp to take him to the location where he had seen the stain.

When they reached the cage that held Joybob and Trixy, there found another stain beneath it. Mr. Microscap examined the stain thoroughly.

It can't be, he thought, then realized what he had to do.

"Have this cage, with the two rats, dispatched to President Skailimet's office immediately. Tell him this is of utmost importance. It is about the Core Fulcrum."

That statement was music to Joybob and Trixy's ears. They were closer to finding the Pivot than ever before.

Goldie, Snowball, Tufty and Katie left the cafeteria together to go for an urgent walk in the botanical garden. Hisky saw them leave together, knew they were planning something, but ignored them. Goldie wanted to discuss his nightmare and the new plans because of it. They reached the Botanical Garden to see Professor Ensure with the sixth-graders near the greenhouse, teaching them about special mushrooms that grew under Banyan trees. They had green-and-red stripes and had special medicinal properties. A bite of the mushroom could heal any wound much faster. Leaving that group behind, they walked to the other side, where many bushes and trees surrounded a small clear lawn. They would have some privacy here. Venus-fly-traps, as large as big cats, decorated one side of the lawn, but they steered clear and sat down in the centre.

Goldie told them all about his nightmare and when he finished Tufty started grinning.

"It was just a nightmare," he said.

"Yes, but I think it was prophetic," said Goldie.

"I agree, sometimes we have realistic dreams. So realistic that they seem to show real events. Even if it is not real, there is no harm in treating it as though it is," said Kattie.

Snowball agreed with her and Tufty relented.

"So, what would you like to do--assuming that the mole-rats have the pivot, or are close to finding it?" Tufty looked at Goldie.

"I assume that they don't have the Pivot yet, or all the magic from our world would have disappeared. I think they are very close to finding it. As you know, Professor Quemarke agreed to let us use a bus to go back to Trapesky after two weeks, but we all think that would be too late," said Goldie.

"Yes, that is true," said Snowball.

"I would like us to target leaving for Trapesky on our own the day after tomorrow morning. We should leave before dawn. It is a weekend, and no one will use the school buses," said Goldie.

"Which bus will we ride?" Kattie asked, a little worried, but in agreement with the plan.

"A falcon. I observed how the pilot operated the controls of the hawk and am sure I can replicate his actions with a falcon," said Goldie.

"I observed it too. A falcon is also one of the quietest and fastest birds in the world, and will be useful in case we need to escape quickly," said Snowball.

"By then we would have completed Dr. Diadoms's training lessons," said Kattie.

"We would also complete one more lesson by Professor Inabaox," added Tufty.

"We will prepare ourselves with the right weapons and tools to face the mole-rat bandicoots. Who knows, we might be back before anyone else wakes up," said Goldie.

"How will we get hold of the keys of the falcon?" Tufty asked.

"That is easy. Mr. Pawsfly--one pilot usually sleeps early, outside his shack beside the anthill. We will borrow them from him. I have seen him hanging those keys on the wall next to his bed," said Snowball.

"Great idea!" They all said and performed high-fives. An adventure was around the corner. Imagine the amazement of all the management members when they came back with the Core Fulcrum? It would be fantastic.

As they continued discussing their plans, talking in whispers, they heard a twig snap from the clearing next to theirs. Someone was nearby.

Oh, oh. Was it Hisky and his gang again? Had he not learnt his lesson by now?

They stood up and walked around the grove of Eucalyptus trees to check. It was not Hisky thankfully. It was Mawgix--the tall, intelligent, black-and-gold, senior *kitdent*. He had a device in his paw and seemed to test it out. The device was a beige-coloured, rubbery container, with a transparent surface filled with a liquid neon-blue gel. The gel contained spots filled with ever-changing, sparkling lights. The device had a thin nozzle in front of it. On the top, there were a few buttons that he clicked constantly, making notes.

Mawgix with the UAC

He looked up and smiled when he saw the little kittens. "Hello there Tufty and Goldie. How are you?"

"Good, thank you. And you?" Tufty greeted him.

"Hello Mawgix. We are well, thank you," said Goldie. "This is my brother-Snowball, and this is my friend Kattie. We are all classmates," he introduced the others to Mawgix.

Mawgix shook paws with all of them.

"Good to see you all here today. Exploring the garden for some class work, I presume?" He asked.

Goldie was not sure if they could discuss their plans with Mawgix so he just nodded.

"What are you testing Mawgix?" Tufty asked, curious about the device in Mawgix's paw.

"Oh this? Remember, I told you a few days back that I am testing a thesis about a Universal Action Controller? This is that device. Its main component is a laser-gel container-and-shooter. When you press this button, it shoots out a laser-gel beam at the target object. The gel binds with the object even if one drop falls on it. Then, with the help of this device, you can control it. There is a microphone here, a joystick here, and a few buttons here with the help of which you can completely control the object. You can either orally communicate with it or via a text message or just move it around with these other controls. This only works on objects smaller than us for the time being. I am working on a larger prototype. Here, let me show you," Mawgix said and moved to the centre of the lawn where a large black ant was scurrying towards a small puddle. It carried a piece of food in its mandibles.

Mawgix carefully aimed the device at the ant and pressed the laser-gel trigger. A very tiny laser beam emanated from the device and hit the ant on its thorax. The ant stopped for a second and looked around, its antennae feeling the surrounding air. Then it continued on its path, accelerating towards its destination. Mawgix spoke into the microphone and the ant stopped again, looking behind it. Then, to the amazement of the kittens, it turned around and walked towards Mawgix, its six legs scurrying forward hurriedly. The senior opened his paw and proffered it to the ant. As he moved the buttons and controls around, the ant dropped the food from its mouth onto Mawgix's paw. It stood there obediently in front of him, waiting for further instructions. After that, Mawgix again spoke through the microphone and pressed some buttons, after which the ant picked up the food from his paw. He pressed a button that cancelled the effect, and the ant was off, on its way to its original destination once more with no memory of what had transpired between them.

"I can use this device on up-to a hundred objects in one filling. This is primarily to restrict its power. With a device of unlimited size, one can cause havoc in this world. The effect wears off after ten minutes, after which the object or being has no memory of its 'controlled' state."

Their excitement knew no bounds. This was the most extraordinary device they had ever seen. They wondered if Mawgix would let them borrow it for their trip to Trapesky.

How will I ask him without revealing the cause? Goldie wondered. He was glad Mawgix trusted them enough to discuss his thesis with them, but the herculean task ahead was to convince him to trust them enough to let them borrow the device for such a risky operation. He thought of testing the waters with Mawgix the next day.

President Skailimet sat in his plush office on the fourth floor of the silver-and-white, presidential mansion. He was a tall, heavy-set, silver-and-grey cat with a mane that extended below his shoulders. He kept the mane hidden in the coat that he usually wore. The large office occupied the central portion of the mansion and had wide bay glass windows behind. Distant, tall mountain ranges graced the scene behind, with skiers on their snow-white slopes, moving upwards in the ski lifts and skiing down the slopes. He was oblivious to the beautiful scenery and garden outside the mansion as he paced the heavily carpeted room. A conference call with the guardians of the Core Fulcrum was in progress.

"It's been over five days since the Core Fulcrum disappeared, and we have made no progress in locating it," he said with resignation.

"We are still trying. Our buses and planes go to different counties every day and scan the locality. We have covered all the counties near Mew Scape and Lussian Peak so far. Now we are widening the net," said Professor Inabaox's voice from the other side.

"This is a question of our credibility. Please let me know what additional support you need, but we cannot afford any more delay. Take my best soldiers and policemen. Use whatever tools, equipment, and resources you want to. Do not leave any stone unturned. As you know, if our enemies locate the Pivot and steal it, we are a doomed race," President Skailimet explained his angst.

"I hear you Skailimet," interjected Professor Quemarke. "This is indeed not only a question of our credibility, but of our survival as a race. We have deployed the best soldiers and equipment for this search. Even the *kitdents* of all the schools have joined us during these operations. Many citizens are trying to help in whichever way they can," he said.

President Skailimet was about to continue when there was a knock on his door.

"President Skailimet, there is an urgent parcel for you." It was his secretary, Ms. Shortpaw.

"Come in," he said, muting the conference Mewline.

Ms. Shortpaw returned shortly and placed a large box in the room on the side bureau.

"It's from Prime Laboratories. Mr. Microscap mentioned it is of utmost importance, relating to the Core Fulcrum," she said.

"Okay. Thank you." He nodded politely but dismissively, and she left the room. He knew Microscap well and trusted his instincts. He unmuted the Mewline once more.

"So, as I was mentioning, we need to try different strategies. One strategy should be to send additional security forces to the Arinelli Mountains and caves near Krusty Dunes desert. Surround the place. If anyone tries to find the Pivot, they will surely reach there first. There is a memorial of the Pivot there. That is the first stop in the quest for the Pivot," he said.

"Hmm, you are right. While we search for the Core Fulcrum, we can ward off anyone who is trying to locate the Pivot. Please start that operation immediately," said Professor Inabaox.

"I will have my best security forces reach Mew Scape to follow your orders," said President Skailimet.

"By the by, what was the reason you had paused in the middle? Is everything all right with the connection on your side?" Professor Quemarke asked. He was very alert about such things.

"I have just received a package from the head of Prime Laboratories -- Mr. Microscap. He says the package is regarding the Core Fulcrum."

Professor Noteworthy's music class was going on in full swing. They made all the instruments used for the music class from natural objects. Billy held his guitar, made from the Lomatia Tinctoria pod and strummed it. Gattino practised on the drum kit made of Wednesday's Wildflowers, Misty played the keyboard made of bamboo shoots, and Melowflues sang a song using a bell flower as a microphone. Together they created a beautiful, mellifluous song called 'All Cats Bright and Beautiful'. Melowflues' voice carried on the wind, stirring everyone who listened. After the first verse, Gattino and Billy joined in for the chorus.

"That was a very good performance," said Professor Noteworthy, singing out the words as usual. I am sure our school has a chance of winning the gold medal in the next Kitaganza music-band contest."

Next to their class, the *kitdents* waited for Professor Inabaox to join them. He was running a few minutes late for the 'Curiosity' class. He apologised profusely when he arrived.

"These are stressful times -- these are. I have to attend several conferences every day. I was engaged in one with both Professor Quemarke and President Skailimet and it went on for a few minutes longer than expected. Let us begin our class for today." He started writing on the board once more. "Today we shall cover the history of the Core Fulcrum and certain aspects of how to become a credible Defender for Eartavista."

Luckily, Goldie, Snowball, Tufty and Katie knew the history part well by now. Any additional information would be a bonus. Professor Inabaox covered all the historical details as per the book they had already read. After that, he started detailing the steps to become a defender.

"As you know by now, the Core Fulcrum gives all of us in Eartavista, powers beyond the ordinary. By us, I mean us -- the cats and kittens. Scientifically, they call us felids and more commonly -- cats or kittens. We need to protect these invaluable powers at all times. The guardians alone cannot achieve this feat. We need citizens to help us too. To formalise this process, we created the Defender program for Eartavista. Any *kitdent* in the sixth or higher grades can formally join the program. Do not confuse this with the current temporary Curiosity Kills the Cat program, which we urgently created because of the current circumstances. There is an entrance test, much like the one we conducted for you all, after which they can join the program. The *kitdents* of this course will get a free pass to that course if interested. The course takes you through multiple levels and teaches you the details about our powers, enemies, defence techniques, governing policies, and many other aspects that are important. You can consider that course as a very detailed version of what I am teaching you. Every year there is an exam held that tests the current skill and capabilities of the defenders. Each *kitdent* starts at the level of 'Defender-0' and rises to the level of a Goldermew. The Goldermew level is the highest achievement for a Defender. The Defenders need to cross levels zero to four to become Goldermews. Most of them fail the last exam, and that is the reason we have such a few Goldermews."

"What is a Fiendyowler?" Snowball asked, biting his tongue as soon as the words escaped from his mouth.

Professor Inabaox froze, wondering from where Snowball had got the information, but dismissively said,

"A Fiendyowler has the same powers as that of the Goldermew; however, it is an evil spirit that works selfishly for itself instead of the good of Eartavista. A Fiendyowler cannot provide Defender training. Only a Goldermew can do that. There are twenty-one Goldermews in the world. A few examples are: President Skailimet, Professor Quemarke and I. There are many others, and, as and when required, I shall introduce their names to you. We do not provide training to become a Fiendyowler."

Professor Inabaox continued looking at Snowball, who looked down immediately. Hisky also stared at him from behind until Snowball felt they were burning a hole into his fur. Goldie gave him a look, but realised he had already learnt from his own mistake.

That evening, Goldie, Snowball, Kattie and Tufty agreed to meet at the Manzar Twins' house to avoid running into other snooping kittens. They would have to lock the door and explain to their parents they were working on a school project together, which was almost true. Their parents would definitely be pleased.

CHAPTER EIGHTEEN

End of Training

King Koresque surveyed the development of the glittering, underground city of Vamoush. After he had given the architect additional coins, the development had sped up considerably. Coins talk, he thought. It looked almost complete. There were several trap systems in place now, and many of those were almost impossible to escape from. The palace's highest point was above the ground, but there was a big moat filled with poisonous dart frogs and electric eels around it. No one would risk approaching the palace directly. They fitted all the royal rooms with skylights, oyster baths, carpets, and Squeaklines. The princesses would be very pleased to move here. They lined all the underground burrows and pathways with glittering enamel. They signed a contract with the world's largest provider of fireflies. These fireflies would provide perennial lighting facilities. Inside the palace, down-feather carpets of the highest quality lined the floors. The eighteen-seater, royal dining room featured a semi-sunken dining room with sea-horses serving the royals their favourite meals. There were over a hundred rooms for the comfort of the royals, and over a hundred helpers at their service at all times. Vamoush itself could house more than a million murids.

Such facilities came at a price. Defence stations surrounded the palace from all sides. There was a high wall with watch towers in every direction. They had made provisions to deploy sophisticated weapons all along the wall to ensure no enemy could approach the palace unseen. If they crossed the barriers and approached the palace, the weapons would strike them down to death almost instantaneously. Most of the city lay underground and undetectable by most of its enemies' radar devices. A dense forest surrounded the external area beyond the wall. Dangerous beings that could kill on sight filled this forest. If they didn't, the hovering guards would finish the task. The dungeons lay far underground as compared to the palace. There was a labyrinth surrounding the dungeons with several traps along the way. As earlier, the only source of light for the dungeons was a central skylight.

There was one more week remaining for the inauguration of the city. All they needed now was the Pivot. He hoped the two musketeers were on the right track. The king was planning to celebrate the inauguration of Vamoush in the assembly ground, in front of the new palace, by destroying the Core Fulcrum in front of his whole kingdom. They would relay that news through all of Murid-land and he would become an immortal figure in their minds. It would be a new start for them--who had suffered long at the hands of the felids. Eartavista required new a new ruler and he would fulfil that requirement.

The radiant cube, locked up in the prison cell, kept sending its distress signals. However, since the carpet and the cage covered it, no one could see them.

President Skailimet opened the parcel to find a cage, with two large motionless mole-rats in it. They appeared to be dead. He threw the cage down in disgust and instructed Ms. Shortpaw to get rid of them. Someone had pranked him. He intended to talk to Microscap later to sort this out. Equally disgusted, his secretary instructed the cleaner to take out the mole-rats and throw them in the garbage bin. The cleaner obliged, and the two mole-rats found themselves on top of a garbage bin outside the president's office.

Joybob sat up as soon as the cleaner left.

"Bleh! Ptui! Ugh!" he said, spitting some disgusting flecks out of his mouth.

Trixy, who had got dumped under a layer of garbage, was even more unlucky. He emerged carrying a broken egg shell on his head, with yellow yolk dripping all over his fur. The shell smelled rotten.

"Yuck, I will pass out here," he said, looking faint.

Joybob punched him hard to bring him to his senses.

"Let's get out of here before someone else puts us into a cage once more," the smart mole-rat said.

"Yes, I can't play dead so many times. It is so hard to hold one's breath," said Trixy.

They jumped out of the bin and ran to the opposite side -- to a river bank. Many yachts stood in the docks.

They looked around in the shops nearby for maps of Krusty Dunes, to check for the river port nearest to it. They found a place called Furrybank and then they found the yacht that would sail in that direction.

Once the kittens reached home, they once more finished dinner quickly and ran upstairs. The smoked crab was one of the best Snowball had ever eaten. They informed their parents that their friends would join them to work on a project. Niamy was glad the twins were engaged in doing constructive work. Paka nodded and buried his face into a magazine. Kattie and Tufty arrived soon after them. After greeting the twins' parents politely, they ran upstairs to join the twins in their room and then locked the door behind themselves. Soon they sat in a circle holding their paws while Goldie clicked on the paw-print. The orb materialised like many times previously, and Dr. Diadoms made an appearance. This time, however, he looked different. For starters, he wasn't smiling.

"Good evening, Dr. Diadoms," said Goldie, excited to start the day's lesson.

Everyone greeted Dr. Diadoms, and he responded politely.

"What will you teach us today?" asked Tufty, equally eager.

"I am afraid I have arrived today to say goodbye -- for the time being." Dr. Diadoms trailed off, with a sombre expression. "It was nice talking to all of you."

"Goodbye? Why? What happened?" Katie wanted to know.

"Inabaox conversed with me this evening, through another book and told me they only allowed this course for *kitdents* enrolled in the Defender program. I agree with him. Unless you are ready to take the course completely, the material could be dangerous."

Goldie could not believe his ears when Dr. Diadoms said that. He looked at Snowball with a look of dread on his face. He knew this was a consequence of what had happened in the class.

"You could talk to Inabaox again and if he doesn't mind, I would be happy to resume the lessons. One must listen to the words of a Goldermew," Dr. Diadoms continued.

Oh, no! Snowball regretted his impulsiveness thoroughly now.

Realizing it was pointless to debate with Dr. Diadoms, they bid him a sad goodbye and exited the orb forthwith. Either they had to convince Professor Inabaox, or stay happy with the two lessons they had received.

One question crept up in Goldie's mind. If Professor Inabaox did not want the fifth-graders to access the book, why had he given the permission to Hisky? Had Professor Inabaox really provided a letter to Hisky for borrowing the book, or was the letter for someone else?

Salmonair, thought Goldie. *Hisky had used his contacts well.*

"I will return this book to the library tomorrow," said Goldie. "No point carrying it around if we may not access this course anymore."

Everyone agreed, although they seemed disappointed.

"Even though we cannot access the rest of the course, I still want to go ahead with the rescue mission. The book has taught us some useful tricks. Kusti and Kedi taught us few effective self-defence techniques and we are better prepared than we were during the previous trip. We will be fine. Tomorrow, we will have our final meeting and plan out all the details of the mission," said Goldie.

"Aye, aye captain," said Tufty.

"Before that important meeting, I would like all of us to arm ourselves with all the useful ingredients and equipment that we have learned about so far. Snowball, Tufty, Kattie, here is what I would like each of you to do..." he whispered his strategy to them.

They swished their tails in surreptitious agreement. The mission was ON.

Joybob and Trixy reached Furrybank early next morning. They ran from the docks to the main centre and grabbed a few crumbs from an empty table at a breakfast eatery, before they saw a bus rumbling into town.

"Let's go, Trixy, our bus is here," said Joybob.

Trixy saw the moving neon label in front of the bus which read Krusty Dunes. He swallowed a few crumbs of cheese and followed Joybob towards the camel-shaped bus. It was one of the bumpiest rides they had ever experienced. As soon as the bus touched the edge of the desert, it turned into a real camel and started plodding over the dunes instead of rolling over it. They kept skidding between seats and almost got stamped on several times by the other passengers, all of whom were in no hurry to go anywhere.

One of the older and fatter felids put her hind leg down on Trixy's tail and sat meowing to the by-sitter for the longest time. Trixy struggled to free his tail from under her leg to no avail. He had to relent and sit down under the seat, bouncing around until she got up. When they arrived at Krusty Dunes, their bodies kept wobbling because of the inertia of traveling in a camel even if the ground under them was stationary. This geographical part of Felid-land was very arid, and there were dunes interspersed with cacti as far as their eyes could see. Their next destination was the Arinelli Mountains.

Now, how were they going to reach that destination? But first, they needed a drink.

On the opposite end of the road was a gas station with an attached shop and café. They bounded towards the station across the seemingly vacant highway and proceeded into the interior of the shop. Soon after, a loud noise distracted them as a car made its way into the enclosure, bursting forth tunes from a radio station. The four young felids appeared as rash as distracted when they stopped to refuel. Joybob's ears picked up the word 'Arinelli' in their conversations with a nearby attendant. They wanted to know how to reach there. Grabbing a drink of water from an abandoned bottle, they sped to the car. Their free ride to the Pivot's location was here.

As soon as Goldie reached school, he walked to the library guided by the usual wasp back from sick leave. Mr. Pustak greeted him politely from behind the central desk, and Goldie requested him to unlock the rear room's

The camel bus to Krusty Dunes

door, which he obliged to politely. Goldie returned the blinking book to its shelf, helped by Essbound. Upon being returned to the shelf, the Secrets' book enthusiastically shook hands with all the neighbouring ones -- who seemed glad to see it back. Goldie -- taken in by the scene, waited a while to watch them and then made his way back to the main hall. He stopped when he saw Mawgix -- seated with his back to him, intently reading a book. The book helped him underline a few words that were too bombastic to comprehend. Goldie thought this was a good time to convince him about using the UAC, without spilling too many beans on the mission itself. He did not want his body to get contorted by disobeying the principles of the NDA.

"Hello Mawgix!" greeted Goldie.

Mawgix looked up at him and greeted him politely -- never irritated about any kind of disturbance. Not only was he intelligent, but was of a pleasant disposition too.

"Hello Goldie, what brings you to the library this morning? Searching for a particular book?" he asked, turning around.

"Yes, I was here to return a book. It was about certain secrets," he said, not wanting to reveal more.

"Was it the book titled 'Secrets of the Core Fulcrum?'"

So, he knew. Goldie felt relieved.

"Yes, that very one, but how do you know about it?"

"Why wouldn't someone like me know about that book? I have read it many times."

"Really? How come?"

"I am a level-two Defender. Next year, I will appear for the level-three exams. I have to know that book like the back of my paw," he grinned sweetly at Goldie.

"But... then... why are you not part of the Curiosity Club?" asked Goldie.

"Not every Defender has joined that mission, but we have our regular duties to protect Eartavista. I was busy with my thesis and the other Defender missions--one of which I will join at Krusty Dunes this afternoon."

Now it all made sense to Goldie. He was not working on his thesis just for the heck of it. It was partly an obligation of his duty towards the world.

"I am amazed by your work on the thesis and humbled by the trust you placed in us," said Goldie earnestly. It was true, Mawgix had shown his magnanimity by entrusting his knowledge in them.

"I knew you were an enlightened *kitdent* as soon as I met you. There is a special sparkle in the eyes of ones enlightened thus. I was not entrusting you; I was helping strengthen Eartavista's defenders."

This was the exact moment Goldie was waiting for.

"If that is the case, I have a request for you. Please, may I borrow your UAC tool for a mission tomorrow? I will return it to you as soon as I am back. I believe the Core Fulcrum is in Trapesky, but Professor Inabaox, and the rest of the management team don't think so. I do not have their backing. However, my belief is that if we delay, we will lose everything dear to us," he rattled out in a single breath.

Mawgix looked at Goldie for a long time and then spoke.

"Come with me. I would like to show you a few things."

They both exited the library to walk towards the kitchen. Then, Mawgix turned to the left and walked along the rear of the swimming pool wall to arrive at the small hostel building. He was not a day scholar. Goldie was aware he was missing Kitdart lessons this morning, but he would make up for it after he completed the mission.

CHAPTER NINETEEN

Equipped and Ready

Snowball waited for Goldie in the indoor stadium where the detailed training for the Balance section of Kitdart was in progress. He touched the side of his bag, where he had stored the special, silver-coloured dust in four different bottles, a combination of both Graphene aerogel and Sparkling Ore dust. He had also collected four big vials of Valerian juice, all from the science lab. The lab assistant had not resisted once he had proven he was 'enlightened'. Tufty had the CLG shots, binoculars, infrared goggles, purple invisibility pellets, listening buds and thermal patches for all of them, in his bag. He had approached Kusti, who was a visiting faculty member, for the equipment, mentioning that it was for the next search mission and that they needed to practise. Kattie had gone to the botanical garden and had collected the special healing mushrooms, lantana petals in small glass jars and some sticky sap from the sticky detention tree in a bottle. Seabreeze too had loaned her a few multi-coloured pellets. One could never know when the need to use them would arise -- especially on a dangerous mission like the one they were about to undertake the next day.

The Arinelli Mountains looked like a place straight out of a scene from The Jungle Book juxtaposed with one from The Arabian Nights. Wild shrubbery grew amidst dense groves of trees, covering the sloping range on the eastern side, while the mountains rose starkly out of the surrounding desert, with several flat-faced cliffs facing the western side. Their surfaces gleamed orange, red, gold and black. The camping site was very close to the Pivot memorial, or so they learnt. Joybob and Trixy jogged up the wild paths until they were very close to the memorial. The felids had cordoned off the whole place by placing grilled gates across all entrance paths. There were half expecting immense security in this place, making it much harder to reach their target destination.

Goldie and Mawgix reached the hostel and walked up the stairs to Mawgix's room on the third floor. His room overlooked the indoor stadium to the right.

Good, thought Goldie. *The others are at Kitdart lessons next door right now. I will soon join them directly from here.*

The room had an attached bath, one bed, a chest of drawers, a cupboard, and a study table. The lone window faced the indoor stadium to the right and to the diagonal left -- the outdoor stadium. Mawgix removed a strange looking gel-filled green square from the top drawer. It had a slot at the top and at the bottom. It had several translucent bubbled compartments that held different ingredients. In addition, there was a microphone and text input panel at the top.

"What is this?" Goldie asked him.

"This is another experiment I am working on. It is a universal dispenser. It is not ready yet but will be in approximately another month. We Defenders need so many objects and ingredients for the various missions that it gets confusing. This universal dispenser has several containers within it. You can input various ingredients into this dispenser, request it for the required final product, and the product will materialize on the output slot. So, all you need to do is carry this one dispenser instead of multiple tools. All the special equipment you need gets produced on-the-go. I am also working on a paw-print recognition interface to make it more secure,"

"This is fabulous! Just what we all need in Eartavista," said Goldie, awed by his creativity.

"Thank you, and now, here is what you were looking for," said Mawgix, handing a gel-filled bulb to Goldie.

"Thank you so much Mawgix. I really don't know how to repay you."

"The success of your mission will be repayment enough," said Mawgix in encouragement.

"Sure, I will remember that. By the way, how does this work?"

Mawgix spent the next ten minutes explaining all the controls to Goldie. Once he had finished explaining, he told Goldie about the science behind the phenomenon.

"This and other devices that bridge the gap between different living-beings or matter work on the concept of gamma rays. Gamma rays are the most energetic form of electromagnetic waves known in the universe. They are at least a thousand times more potent than visible light rays and yet they have the shortest wavelengths. A light ray's wave is at least a million times longer than a gamma ray's wave."

"Wow, I did not know that," said Goldie. It was an eye-opening experience to understand the details behind extraordinary phenomena.

Mawgix continued, "Every object emits these rays under certain circumstances. We, for instance, emit at least six-hundred gamma rays with every thought we have. The work on this is still premature, but every civilization on this planet has explored this aspect. The energy fields around matter contain these rays, bound in energy fields. Some beings call this invisible spiritual energy Orenda, others call it Chi, or Aura. These energies all point to the same concept related to gamma rays. They are the building blocks of a universal code between all kinds of matter, whether living or non-living. In recent studies, scientists closely examined beings with telekinetic powers. They discovered them releasing bursts of gamma rays at the time when their power peaked, and they moved objects. I have explored this very aspect to create these tools with great success. A detailed understanding of the language of these energies gives us greater control and extraordinary powers. Traditional science teaches us about physical dimensions that are very limited in number. Energy science teaches us about the unlimited dimensions of energy that exist, of which most of us can fathom only a few. Once you open your mind, the sky is the limit."

Goldie continued discussing the topic with Mawgix for a few more minutes. He vowed to himself to work with Mawgix on his projects going forward as he could gain significant knowledge from this wise senior. Then, when it was getting late, he departed after wishing him luck for his Defender mission. Mawgix also started packing equipment since he would leave shortly. When Goldie reached the indoor stadium, the session was almost over, so he just sat down at the edge and watched the others complete their training. Hisky was the top scorer of the day, followed by Kattie and Cica. Hisky looked happier than he had for many days before.

After the Kitdart session, Goldie, Snowball, Tufty and Kattie huddled together again in the near the fountains. A few kittens from kindergarten played with their classmates on the other side. They looked like tiny balls of fur of different colours, dotting the fresh grass. The teacher threw a large ball of twine in the air, and they launched themselves at it before it hit the ground, grabbing it with their tiny claws, their ears held back in tame aggression, gnawing and biting it, while kicking hard on its surface with their tiny hind feet, until they all rolled around with it several times. It was all fun for their class teacher and entertainment for whoever watched.

"So, here is what I am suggesting. Tomorrow, we will meet at four a.m. beside the school's parking zone. Snowball, you will grab the key from Mr. Pawsfly and meet us near the parked falcons. We will fly to Trapesky, get the Core Fulcrum and return before sunrise if possible. Carry satchels for all the equipment we will need. We must fully equip ourselves with all the tools. Also, let us inform Billy to inform Professor Inabaox in case we do not return before sunset. We just have to tell him we are going on a secret mission to Trapesky. Nothing more," Goldie instructed them all.

They agreed on all the plans and then divided the equipment in equal parts, except for the UAC, which only Goldie carried.

The guard - who stood next to the memorial in Arinelli, thought he saw the grass move in the clearing under him and stared at it for a long time, however, the grasshopper moved away to another patch.

Bah, he thought. *There are no intruders here, but the stress of weeding out minor pests is killing me under this sweltering heat.*

He, along with twenty other guards, stood in front of the Pivot memorial, which enshrined a gigantic rhombicosidodecahedron, made of the hardest, blackest and shiniest galaxy-granite in the world. A huge plaque in front of the memorial detailed the history of the Pivot and the chronology of the construction and inauguration of the memorial. There were several miniatures in glass boxes, on top of pedestals around it, in different shades of black and grey. Those miniatures were creations by felid scientists through historical ages, to replicate the Pivot. The cases contained labels detailing the year of its creation and the name of the scientist. The memorial stood in centre of the main cave inside the tallest peak in the Arinelli mountain range. A few tourists moved along its interiors, reading about the details of each stone. The security guards

Joybob burrows under the Pivot

admitted them only after a thorough examination of their bags and selves.

Under the pedestal, Joybob and Trixy were at work. Luckily, all these pedestals were hollow and made of termite resistant wood, which stood directly on the ground. *How inane*. The duo had special teeth that could dig and drill through mud or wood at breakneck speed. They worked hard, moving upwards until they hit a surface; it was a thick layer of wood.

Mawgix reached the Arinelli memorial site along with Salmonair, Seabreeze and a few others. They were all on duty based on the orders received by President Skailimet. They had to make sure they caught any 'strange' intruders near the site. After a discussion amongst themselves, they wore thermal patches and infrared goggles to scan the clearing in front of the entrance of the memorial. Everything seemed under control.

The whole day passed by in a blur for Goldie and the gang. After their discussion on the lawn, they attended the Languages class, during which Professor Neko talked about the various accents of cats from around the world.

"Cats from the central part of Eartavista say Meowr (note the extra 'R' in the meowing) as opposed to the ones from the central or eastern zones. Eastern cats use the 'R' sound sparingly. Their meows are higher in pitch as compared to the ones from the rest of the world. Western cats emphasize the first syllable of every word they speak. One must know these differences to communicate properly." Ms. Neko showed them an interactive map and pressed different locations in Eartavista to play the various accents. "For next week, I would like you all to plan a few skits with characters from each of these zones and speak with the correct accents. You will get bonus points for using props and costumes," she said.

Hisky imagined himself as a king from central Eartavista addressing two handcuffed peasants called Goldie and Snowball, '*Rambunctious rogues. Get rid of them straightaway*', he commanded.

The four were too excited about the mission to think about the skit; However, they put it on their important task list.

The mathematics class also sped by as though the relative speed of time was directly proportional to the proximity of an adventure. Professor Manimore's realistic trains showed concepts of speed, distance, and time better than anything else could. At the end of the session, she asked the class a riddle as she was wont to do.

"There are two trains moving towards each other on the same track. One train's speed is forty kilometres an hour, and the other train's speed is sixty kilometres an hour. The distance between them, when they start, is a hundred kilometres. There is a bee between them that travels at a speed of twenty kilometres an hour. It buzzes towards one train, touches it, then turns to buzz in the opposite direction until it touches the opposite train and so on... By the time the trains meet, how many kilometres would the bee have travelled?"

Pompom had a straight answer,

"Should be zero, Ma'am. Won't it buzz away long before it touches any train?"

Everyone chuckled in response. The actual solution to the riddle was twenty kilometres, answered correctly by Goldie.

As the end of the day drew nearer, their excitement became palpable. According to their plan, they informed Billy, Clawcia and Melowflues about their trip to Trapesky on a secret mission, without revealing the actual details of the trip. They told them to inform Professor Inabaox if they did not return by sunset the next day. Although the three of them looked worried, they did not ask them for more details since they assumed it was about a mission concerning the Core Fulcrum. They knew about the Core Fulcrum and its disappearance thanks to the news.

When the sun set on the Arinelli mountains, the guards and Defenders started leaving as new ones arrived for new shifts. Mawgix, Salmonair and Seabreeze also departed. The orders from the top were to continue keeping watch in shifts until they found their magical cube. Basker -- the guard, felt relieved. Nothing had gone wrong during his shift. They had checked all the tourists visiting the premises thoroughly. Their checks had revealed nothing. No malevolent beings had dared to venture anywhere near the monument. He walked a final time around the circumference of the central pillar to check if everything was fine. It was. As he shut the gates to the memorial and museum, he thought of one of the miniature Pivots behind. It had looked darker and smoother than usual. *Hmm, he had never noticed such smoothness before. However, it had not shifted from its position in the glass case, and that was the most important thing.*

CHAPTER TWENTY

Kitdents on a Mission

Before dawn could strike, the four were up and ready with their satchels, filled with equipment. They had enlisted the help of squirrel buggies for their transportation to school the previous day. Now, they bounded through trees, scurried over roads, climbed over buildings and ran through meadows, until they rounded the corner, to reach the enormous clearing that housed their school. Through the nipping fog, they barely saw its form rising silently. The machinery under the school was at work, whirring and churning, to change its structure before sunrise. Royal cat structures rose higher, turned around and descended lower, rotating on invisible plates. Shivering and chattering under their coats, they ran to the area near the parking zone, where there stood mini tenements of the school's blue-collar staff. Goldie, Kattie and Tufty ran to the row of falcon gliders to wait, while Snowball slunk towards the tall anthill, behind which, lived their target.

They watched with bated breath as he reached the mini townhouse, outside which, Pawsfly slept on a pallet. His snores filled the air like a swarm of gigantic bees, revving up their wings, followed by a whistling pause. Snowball slowly crept around the bed to approach the brick wall behind, where Pawsfly had hung the key-holder. There, he found the key with an attachment in the shape of a falcon's head with the number 'Falcon02' engraved in it. The falcon had eyes made of white beads, and a blue-and-white plumage. As soon as Snowball grabbed the key in his jaws, the eyes lit up, and in a squawking tone, the key said,

"Face unrecognised. INTRUDER ALERT, INTRUDER ALERT."

With apprehension rising within, Snowball stuffed the key in his mouth, trying to shut out the sound. Having done that, he bounded as fast as he could to his waiting gang. The key kept buzzing inside. He had not expected this level of security. Luckily, all Pawsfly did was turn over and resume snoring. Hopefully, he would still be asleep when they returned the key to the key holder, later that morning. They ran to the glider having the same registration number as the key and opened it. The key was still buzzing loudly, but worked all the same. Snowball leapt into the pilot's seat and turned the key in the slot for the engine. The others strapped themselves into the passenger seats. The engine started revving, and the glider converted itself into a flapping falcon. The controls were simple, and though the falcon swooped up and down for a while, soon Snowball got the gist of it, and they were smoothly airborne -- flying speedily in Trapesky's direction with the help of the compass onboard.

With just four days to spare, Joybob and Trixy finally brought the Pivot stone to Trapesky. They had selected the blackest amongst the miniatures as their target. Burrowing had worked again. Trixy held the black gleaming stone in a sack on his back, as they trudged down the well to the secret trapdoor. With dawn yet awaited, darkness enveloped the passages, making it difficult to speed up. The underground chamber was empty as they made their way to the right, from where they had seen King Koresque emerge on the first day. Two spear-yielding guards blocked the way to the door.

"Hark! Who goes there?" One guard said, as their spears crossed the diagonals of the mullioned door.

"Hey, it's cool. It's just us, the super-cool, smart, undercover spies of Trapesky. We have a gift for the king. He will be mighty pleased," said Joybob, pointing to the sack on Trixy's back.

"What is it?" asked the other guard severely, his long moustache almost covering his mouth. On speaking, it gave the appearance of him trying to nibble it.

"It's the Pivot, remember? Were you there during that first meeting when we showed him a gleaming cube? The king had asked us to retrieve the Pivot -- its antidote. We have achieved that task. Now, please let us meet him quickly. He might reward you two also, you know," continued Joybob.

The two guards exchanged glances and imperceptible gestures of silent communication before deciding to allow them inside. One of them opened the padlock and entered the passage to escort the duo inside.

"Why did you directly not access the palace via the marbled staircase?" he asked, as he led the way.

"The king has forbidden us spies from ever using the front entrance. We are always engaged in confidential missions which warrant secrecy," said Trixy.

The guard led them to a circular waiting chamber, which although not as stark and dank as the first one, was definitely not the epitome of luxury either. There were planks and pigeon holes attached to the walls around, providing the appearance of makeshift sitting racks or rather -- discussion benches. One lone window provided some light in the room, and scarlet, translucent drapes adorned that window. A spiral staircase ascended from that room upwards.

"Please wait here," the guard said as he ascended the stairway.

Joybob and Trixy followed him with their eyes until he disappeared into the dark, yawning hole in the ceiling. The king and his two ministers followed the guard down in sometime, his one eye gleaming, heralded by the news he had just heard. The two bowed down low in greetings and subjugation to him.

"Where is the Pivot -- the elusive object I have coveted for so long?" he asked once he was in the circular chamber. Trixy handed the sack to him. The King opened the sack and beheld the blackest stone he had ever seen. Its many glittering surfaces reflected his one-eyed visage. He retrieved some sparkling dust from a pouch inside his pocket and as they watched, sprinkled some glittery dust on it. Light rays from the dust slowly got attracted to the black stone until they got absorbed in it, leaving behind just grey ash. "Yes! This must be it!" he said with devious approbation.

Joybob and Trixy twitched their noses and whiskers with quivering happiness. Relief washed all over them. They could have cried tears of joy right then.

Removing a bag of coins from the pocket inside his cloak, the king handed it to both of them.

"You have pleased me. Take these coins and do what your hearts want to with them. Go where your free spirits might take you," he said. "However, in four days, present yourselves at the inauguration of Vamoush, when I plan to destroy the Core Fulcrum in front of my whole kingdom! I am sure you would want to watch too."

He placed the stone in the same pocket whence he had removed the bag of coins. He had the magical cube and the Pivot. Now murids would rule the world. Joybob and Trixy gladly accepted the coins and ran, intending never to return.

Soon the falcon piloted by Snowball was flying by the seashore along the marble-faced cliffs near Trapesky. The cliffs gleamed silvery-white under the setting moonlight. They passed the extensive and dense forest, approaching the clearing next to the ruins, keeping the falcon in glide mode as they scanned the surroundings for mole-rat warriors. This time, there were several of them posted on treetops and walking in the clearing. They definitely did not want a repeat of the last episode.

"All -- please drink Valerian juice, we are going to war!" said Snowball, and promptly all of them took a sip of the juice.

"Ready your infrared goggles, thermal patches, binoculars, listening buds and CLG shots. We need to get rid of those bandicoot rats below us if we plan to land," said Goldie.

Having followed the instructions as per Snowball's announcement, they now peered through their binoculars and took aim with their CLG shots. Goldie aimed at two mole-rats stationed on top of the trees in the forest. His shots found their targets, and they collapsed, hanging from the upper-most branches. Kattie took aim at the mole-rats walking about in the clearing and successfully made them pass out too. Tufty found a few of them around the well -- near the ruins and hit them accurately. Snowball did a sweep of the area a few times at varying heights to see if there were any more threats. Having found none, he flew the falcon down, to land on the clearing next to some thick palm trees. After landing, he moved the vehicle further into the forest, so it was amidst foliage and looked camouflaged. He put the buzzing key under the pilot's seat's cushion, and it promptly stopped the noise.

"Now, quick! Let us all go towards the well. Be alert! Those warriors could approach us from any direction!" said Goldie.

With two of them leading the way, they looked in all four directions while walking in a group to ensure there were no surprises sprung on them. They passed the unconscious warriors as they headed towards the ruins. There was no one else about. They were careful to avoid either stepping on the path made of grass or the toadstools, as they made their way to the well.

One must let sleeping spiders lie, thought Goldie.

Just as they were about to descend the steps adjoining the well, the lantana petals in Tufty's jar took on the shape of a mole-rat, betokening approaching enemy forces. Sure enough, two snickering and happy-looking mole-rats emerged from the bottom of the well. The kittens caught them by surprise as they walked over the well's edge. Quickly reacting, Goldie and Snowball attacked them with their extended claws, and both the mole-rats collapsed--falling on top of thick lotus leaves in the well. There they floated, while frogs croaked at them indignantly for ousting them from their leafy thrones. The four kittens made their way down the steps gingerly. They were on high alert for more danger ahead. The next moment, Tufty's thermal patch started heating, and he quickly looked up behind him to see two of them taking aim at the group with spears from the top of the well. Tufty and Kattie's CLG shots found their marks, and they plunged headlong, squeaking loudly, into the well's depths and got stuck in the hyacinth. Their spears fell into the water next to them. The four now reached the bottom step of the well, and except for the big daffodil bush adjoining the wall, the layer of water beneath, and the circular wall all around, they could see nothing.

"Where did they emerge from? There must be a secret door here. On the other day too, several warriors had emerged from the well. Where there's a well, there's a way," said Goldie, almost rhetorically.

Just then, a large daffodil turned to them and requested sweetly, "Password please?"

"Wait - what?" The unexpected request took everyone by surprise.

"Password please?" she repeated, her countenance a picture of sweet composure.

Many ideas raced through Goldie's mind, but he dismissed them. Then he asked Kattie and Snowball, "What did Professor Inabaox say was Trapesky's ruler's name? Tufty and I were quite... um... occupied with copying the book-of-secrets during that session."

They both wracked their brains for some time before Kattie answered. "Koresque. King Koresque," she exclaimed.

As soon as she said that, a yawning passage opened behind the bush.

"You may now enter," said the daffodil, pleasantly.

"Well, I would never --," said Goldie, before bending his head to walk into the dark and creepy passage. The others followed him in, after which the trapdoor shut behind them. The passage was dimly lit because of less lighting. There were only a few scattered lanterns -- no doubt made of glow worms. However, even by that light, they saw it -- the splattered, glittering stardust all over the interior of the rocky corridor.

"See this, Snowball, Tufty, Kattie, we were right!" whispered Goldie. "The Core Fulcrum is here somewhere."

The kittens fight the mole-rats

"I wonder how they cleaned the exterior of all the tell-tale signs? Could they have sourced venom from the giant spider?" asked Snowball, whispering in the dark. He quickly collected some star dust into an empty bottle. As they walked along, they arrived at a large vacant underground chamber. There was a makeshift rocky throne at the other end. To the rear of the chamber, the pathways split to the left and the right. The glimmering star dust coated the walls to the left.

"This is an interesting looking chamber, maybe this is where King Koresque held his meetings for all his underhand activities," said Snowball.

"Keep yourselves alert, this is no time for any other thoughts. Let us follow the trail to the left," said Goldie, keeping his CLG shot ready.

They took the path to the left, and as soon as they rounded the bend on it, a spear came flying at them and grazed Tufty's shoulder.

"Ouch!" he said, as big drops of blood trickled down.

"Eat the mushroom, Tufty!" said Kattie, as Goldie and Snowball barged into the path and sent a volley of CLG shots at the mole-rat bandicoots in the corridor. The enemy mole-rats shuddered vigorously as the shots successfully felled them to the floor. Tufty ate the piece of mushroom that Kattie offered him, and the wound vanished within a few seconds, like it had never existed.

Thoroughly shaken, the kittens proceeded the rest of the way in complete silence, scanning back and forth to ensure they no one was targeting them. The left path descended a flight of stairs and then suddenly turned to the right. They could discern some light at the end of that corridor, which they assumed was because of an opening or a skylight. There could be mole-rats waiting there to ambush them. Gingerly stepping on the rocky floor, to not make any sound, they walked ahead one step at a time. Soon they were at the grilled door that separated them from the lit area. They waited for a few minutes, holding their breath behind the door, in case it would get opened by someone from the other side. They saw no movement and heard no sound for a long time. Convinced that they had shot everyone, they pushed the door open slowly, to step out into the huge circular garden.

What a beautiful atrium it was! It was one like they had never seen before. Beautiful and fragrant flower bushes adorned a well-manicured garden. There were at least a score variety of trees heavily lining the garden. In between the carpet of grass, they found ponds and sand pits. It was a veritable paradise. The skylight above comprised gel-like, transparent spheres, supported on thick, white-coloured ropes laid out like a bulging grid on the roof. That structure scattered rays of light into softer concentric circles, which made tessellated patterns around the garden. So taken in were they with the sight, that they did not notice a net descend on them, gather them into a tight heap, and lift them above the ground, such that they flailed their arms and dropped their CLG shots into the bushes below them.

* * *

CHAPTER TWENTY-ONE

Escape from the Dungeons

Billy could not sleep well. He tossed and turned in his hammock, hung from floating trees, outside the shack they lived in. Somehow, he felt it was not right for Goldie, Snowball, Tufty and Kattie to proceed by themselves to Trapesky -- a potentially dangerous location with no backup -- although they had bantered about it. He did not know the details of their mission, but was sure it was about the Core Fulcrum. He used the Mewline to awaken Clawcia and Melowflues. Maybe they could put together a standby rescue team. Clawcia luckily kept an extension right next to her bed and awakened as soon as he called. He told Clawcia to call Melowflues. When Clawcia called Melowflues, her mother answered instead, in the same high-pitched and sweet voice that her daughter had inherited. They agreed to meet in the next thirty minutes at school. Only cricket buggies were available before aurora, so he reluctantly boarded one -- trying to ignore the feeling of weightlessness as it took large parabolic leaps forward. When he reached school, Clawcia and Melowflues had already assembled.

As they walked towards Professor Quemarke's quarters next to the school, they saw two senior *kitdents* running towards the school parking ground. One was a tall black-and-gold kitten, and the other was a petite white-and-blue one. The latter had a windswept, light-blue mane behind her neck. They were Mawgix and Seabreeze, both of whom were bounding towards a hawk. On a whim, these three ran towards them, to inform them and get some urgent, well-needed help. The seniors incidentally were in fact headed to Trapesky themselves. Melowflues, who rode the same bus as Seabreeze, requested the seniors to take them along. After much cajoling, they agreed. However, since the juniors had had no training in weapon usage or Defence Arts, the seniors asked them to stay in the hawk with glue shots -- claw-shaped guns that shot out sticky glue onto the unsuspecting targets. Senior Defenders underwent training in operating various school buses so they were in safe paws. Mawgix started the hawk smoothly, and it took off into the sky, soon sailing high above the landscape.

Far away, at Trapesky, the kittens tried to contort themselves to reach the equipment in their furry satchel bags -- in vain. The more they struggled, the tighter the net bound itself around them. However, even if they could access the equipment, whom would they target? No one stood below or around them in the garden, as they swung suspended from a palm tree. They were in a lot of trouble. Snowball's whole life started flashing in front of him. He thought of his parents -- whom he had not even hugged goodbye in the morning. Tufty thought of all the times he had spent pranking his brother and wished to ask him for forgiveness. Kattie thought of the gymnastics world championship title, which she had vowed to herself, she would win. Goldie thought of the mission and the irony of their situation. Finally, they heard a voice.

"Welcome, felids, welcome. It sure is an honour to host you in our kingdom. You have arrived at an opportune time," it said.

They looked around wildly to locate the source of the voice, and finally, they saw a group of mole-rats emerge out of the same entrance they had used for admittance into the garden. The forerunner of them was the king, and he looked exactly as Goldie had imagined. From this close, he was even more ugly.

"We have the Core Fulcrum; we have the Pivot and now we have you. What a fantastic combination!" the king clapped, looking up at them as he said that. The other guards snickered and clapped behind him. By then, all the guards had recovered since the CLG shot only worked as a temporary tranquillizer. They absentmindedly rubbed their necks and behinds to numb the strange sensation.

He had the Pivot? Can't be! Thought Goldie, with indignation and apprehension.

"You possess the Pivot in your dreams --you LIARS AND THIEVES!" shouted Snowball. "Wait till I get my claws on you-- SCUMS OF EARTAVISTA!"

On account of the fine mesh around them, he could not elongate his claw, without it getting stuck. Goldie gave him a look to stop.

"Hmm. I am afraid the opportunity has passed," the king said dolefully to Snowball, as he removed the black stone from his pocket and showed it to everyone. The gleaming stone seemed to turn any glimmering particles into ash. Rejoicing at the expression of the kittens, he then addressed his guards, "Take their fallen weapons, and throw them into a prison cell. Let them stay hungry until they learn to have more respect for us. We will eliminate them as soon as we destroy their cube in front of them." Then, with a glint of his wicked teeth and a sweep of his cloak, he departed.

Since their small cross-body satchels were furry, they remained camouflaged under them. The guards -- there were several of them by then, lowered the net -- still tightly wrapped around them, and pushed them into a prison cell next to the one occupied by the Core Fulcrum. After that, convinced that the young felids were now innocuous in their unarmed state, they collected the four CLG shots and vanished down the corridor, leaving behind Chooha and Vermish to monitor the whole area. The king needed help for the preparations of the move to Vamoush from most of the guards. As expected, Vermish and Chooha posted themselves right opposite their cell, taking turns for breaks as needed.

The hawk reached Trapesky within an hour's time. They circled around the marble cliffs a few times to understand its layout better. Then Clawcia's sharp eyes spotted the white patch amongst the trees.

"Is that a school glider? I remember Snowball mentioning that they were planning to take a falcon glider," she pointed to the falcon -- almost completely camouflaged under the trees.

"It looks like one to me. Should we land next to it?" asked Melowflues, almost unable to contain her excitement.

"Could be. However, it would be dangerous to land near it at the wrong time," Mawgix said.

"When will we know it is right?" asked Billy. He was eager to rescue his friends.

"They are here for a mission, and we want to make sure we don't interfere with it. However, if they do not emerge soon, we may have to go after them," said Mawgix.

"Let us keep an eye out for enemies and deal with them in the meantime. Hopefully, that will be a big help for their mission," said Seabreeze, as she gazed out through her binoculars.

Soon enough, they saw mole-rats emerging out of a well to walk towards the beautiful palace. They were busy conversing about something and seemed unaware of the hawk above until one of them suddenly looked up and noticed them. He soon gestured upwards, at which point they started taking aim at the bird with their spears and bows-and-arrows.

"Uh-oh, action time," said Mawgix looking at Seabreeze. The seniors did not want the mole-rats to create a pandemonium and jeopardise the mission.

They removed ultraviolet-lavender-freeze guns and shot the guards. The guards froze on the spot in different positions -- some of them still connected to their weapons with an icy streak. They were all covered in neon-lavender-coloured ice.

"Ha, ha, ha! I love these fast weapons. It feels like a game of freeze with authentic effects," said Mawgix, performing the high-five with Seabreeze while the juniors watched in awe. All mole-rats that emerged from the well ended up with the same fate.

"Hurry Goldie, these statues will melt soon, although they will not remember what had hit them," said Seabreeze.

They moved the hawk further away from the clearing to avoid raising further alarm.

Kattie used her sharp claws to cut through the mesh behind her. She hastened the sawing motion whenever the mole-rats looked away. The mole-rats were initially tenacious; However, after an hour of taking turns to stare at the mesh heap in the cell, the fatigue started to show. The first sign was a yawn by the tall, fat one--Vermish, followed by a stretch of the forearms by the short, thin one--Chooha. Kattie sped up the cutting. The others, getting the hint, joined her. They wriggled, then stopped, then wriggled again and then stopped again. It was akin to playing peek-a-boo with a twist. They got better with time. Soon, the holes were large enough for them to reach for their satchels. Goldie whispered a plan into their ears. He had a strong conviction that the Core Fulcrum was in one neighbouring cell, since he had seen stardust scattered all around the garden.

Vermish yawned again and departed for his lunch break, letting Chooha stay behind to guard the prisoners. He would return shortly and then let Chooha proceed for his meal. Chooha too was tired of staring into the cell and couldn't wait to dig his teeth into some delicious cheese. His stomach was growling. *Umm*. He stretched his legs and peered into the cell. The heap looked distinctly smaller. Rubbing his eyes, he stood up to investigate. Pressing his face into the bars as much as he could, he began to count the felids in the net once more. As he did that, the bunch-of-keys from his pocket magically rose in the air and moved into the cell. It was a like a ghost had possessed it. Just as he was digesting this incredulously, a claw reached all the way from the heap and scratched him across his cheek.

"Aargh!" he said, staggering backward. At once, the bunch-of-keys floated out of the cell, guided by an invisible force and turned a few keys in the lock, until one of them opened the door. Alarmed by this, Chooha quickly picked up his spear. "STOP! Stop or I will harm you!" he said, pointing his spear towards the cowardly ghost that dared not show itself. To his surprise, neither his quivering voice nor his shivering legs matched the brave intention of his thoughts. The 'ghost' pulled the spear from his paws and threw it out of reach into the quicksand. Chooha saw it sinking slowly. Now he was completely frightened. "Wh... who are you? Wh... why can't I see you? Are you... you (gulp) a ghost? I... I am not... not a... afraid of you!" he chattered, picking up a wobbly stick and pointing it at the keys that were now rotating around him. After a few rotations with the keys, the claw struck from the heap again. The gash drew enough blood to make him pass out immediately.

A bunch of keys floats out of Chooha's pocket

Goldie, who was the 'ghost' had consumed a purple pellet to become invisible. Now he freed the others from the net. They found a few leaves to stuff into the mesh instead and ran out. They bounded clockwise around the prison cells looking for their target -- the Core Fulcrum. The other prisoners -- who had watched the drama unfold in front of them, clapped and cheered. The kittens released all of them one by one as they passed them, and the prisoners escaped happily. The four had almost completed their circuit around the garden, when they arrived at a cell that was right next to theirs in the anticlockwise direction. There they saw a cube-like object covered with a carpet hovering in a cage. With triumphant exhilaration, Goldie opened the cell door and ran inside. The others followed close on his heels. The object too made its way to the door of its cage, as through recognising its saviour.

It was almost noon when Professor Quemarke received an urgent call on his Mewline. His face grew pale after the conversation and he summoned Professor Inabaox from the staff room. When he arrived, they had a sombre conversation.

"I have bad news for you. Not one, but two. Which one would you like to listen to first?"

Professor Inabaox looked worried. "Tell me either, Professor Quemarke."

"The first is that a miniature Pivot went missing yesterday evening from the Arinelli site, and the second one is that several fifth-grade students have borrowed a falcon. They are now at Trapesky. I am guessing it is the group that met us in my office three days ago. What is the name of their leader -- the golden kitten? I think it's Goldie."

"Correct. Who stole the Pivot?"

"Intelligence points to mole-rat bandicoots."

"How did they steal it with so much security around? We had guards and Defenders protecting the monument round the clock."

"These were brilliant and dangerous bandicoots. They took the darkest Pivot miniature by burrowing under it. We need to upgrade infrastructure and security for all the heritage and precious monuments in Eartavista. However, first, you need to rescue those *kitdents*. They may be in grave danger."

A while later, another falcon left the school parking zone, with Professor Inabaox, Kusti and Kedi in the passenger seats. They had armed themselves with the required weapons.

Goldie fumbled with the bunch of keys to find the one that would unlock the cage, but none worked. Frustrated, the four kittens tried all means of breaking it, to no avail. After coming so far, this lock had them stymied. Just then, they heard a squeaky scream outside. On running out, they saw Vermish bent over Chooha's bruised body -- shock written all over his face. His wriggling ears grew pink with consternation.

"Chooha! SQUEAK! Who did this to you? Where are all the prisoners?" Vermish tried to shake him into consciousness. Chooha did not budge.

"Where is the key to the Core Fulcrum's cage?" asked Snowball from behind him -- his claw drawn.

Vermish whipped around to see three felids and a floating bunch of keys, which he presumed were the ones stolen from Chooha. At full height, the mole-rat bandicoot was taller than them, but his eyes showed fear. He put his paw around the rear pocket of his pants to shield it. Getting the hint, Snowball struck his pocket with his claw, and a key bunch dropped out. As the mole-rat opened his mouth in alarm, Tufty threw sticky-tree gel on it. As expected, it sealed shut completely, only allowing the output of muffled sounds.

"AFA MAFFA KIRR ICH," said Vermish, pointlessly trying to screech loudly as Tufty stuck his paws together using the same gel.

"Now you will be as useful as your friend here," said Tufty, pointing to Chooha, pleased with his job.

In the meantime, Goldie -- still invisible, took the new bunch of keys and bounded inside the cell once more. Within seconds, he released the Core Fulcrum from the cage, and a burst of twinkling light escaped from the cell. The kittens felt a new explosion of energy surge through them, which almost threw them backwards. The divine cube raced out of the cell and hovered -- pulsating with radiance in front of them. At that very moment, they heard a roar from above them. The bubbled-roof opened up like a can to reveal a hideous monster. It was the giant, green, trapdoor spider. They heard screams from outside as it stomped on the escaping prisoners and threw them onto the bubbled roof. They got stuck on its sticky surface. The spider took advantage of their immobility and stung them with its sharp jaws. The glass bubbles on the roof were actually its eggs mixed with foam, and the grid of ropes was its lair. One of the exiting prisoners would have awakened it by sitting on the toadstools. *Oops*.

CHAPTER TWENTY-TWO

Freedom at Last

"Quick -- everyone, arm yourselves with the Valerian Laser Power. Please place your paws on the top of the cube," shouted Goldie over the roar, while the confused, frightened mole-rat looked on. They all did as instructed. Exactly as per the book and the training lesson, beams of light projected out of the cube, pierced through their paws, spilt over like lava and disappeared like snowflakes around them. Vermish almost collapsed in shock at the sight.

"MYAW HAW VALERIAN JUICE!" exclaimed Snowball, performing a flip in the air. He almost couldn't believe it.

Kattie stared at her paw like she was in a dream. Tufty had to pinch himself too.

"Now everyone, be very careful about this power. Use this power sparingly and when most necessary," said Goldie wondering how to take the cube out of the garden.

Snowball had another idea. He brought the meshed net out of the cell they were in before and wrapped it around the cube. "Let's walk out through the entrance. Keep the cube in between."

Goldie and Tufty led the way, holding the mesh from behind them. Snowball and Kattie followed them. The cube dutifully hovered in between. Kattie gave Vermish a parting swipe with her claw, and he collapsed next to Chooha.

Mawgix and Seabreeze circled around the palace to return to the ruins, and what a scene awaited them! A gigantic spider rampaged through the clearing, stomping on anything and everything in its way. It threw many animals towards a large trapdoor which had opened up and bit them when they got stuck on the sticky pearls. The deadly bite caused the animals to become unconscious. This spider was too big for either the UAC or the freeze guns. They did not have CLG shots, hence had to think of something else quickly. Mawgix turned to the junior *kitdents*.

"This is the time you can help. Aim your glue shots at the feet of the spider. Shoot as many times as you want," he said.

Excited to help, Billy, Clawcia and Melowflues launched a torrent of glue shots at the monstrous spider's feet. However, because of their lack of training, their aims were not accurate, and the shots landed in the wrong locations. Mawgix flew the hawk lower and closer to the spider's legs to make it easier for the *kitdents* to aim well. The proximity helped, and soon the shots started finding their marks. One by one, the spider's legs got thoroughly glued to the ground below it. It screeched and roared in frustration at the loss of its mobility.

"Now aim for its jaws," said Mawgix as he made the hawk soar upwards. That was a mistake. The spider, angry with the flying bird, caught it firmly in its large jaws. Its sharp mandibles pierced through the surface of the bio-mechanical glider, as it tried to crush them.

Below them, over a thousand mole-rats spilled out of the palace and surrounding areas, holding formidable weapons of all kinds, followed by a royal looking mole-rat bandicoot, seated on a gigantic scorpion, inside a glass bubble. He held a special weapon that looked like a metallic dandelion. It was King Koresque.

The four made their way through the passage, encountering several soldiers that wanted to stop them from escaping with the cube. They clawed their way through all of them. Kattie used the lasso trick on a few of them. When they emerged from the trapdoor in the well, they beheld a frightening sight above them. A hawk from their school hung from the jaws of the gigantic spider. On closer look, it contained Mawgix, Seabreeze and their friends. The glider swung precariously from its jaws a hundred metres above them, while the spider tightened its grip with its mandibles, slowly contorting the metallic frame. Mawgix and Seabreeze kept aiming lavender shots at its jaws, which froze a few of its teeth, but was not enough to stop its mandibles. Billy and Clawcia fired glue shots into its mouth, which were ineffective because of the cancelling effect of its venom. Melowflues screamed loudly as she predicted a horrific ending. Goldie -- who was visible by then, thought it was time to attack.

"Friends, the time has come for me to use the Valerian Laser Power. HOLD ON," he said as he closed his eyes and thought of the cube in all its glory. He took aim at the spider's head, saying Valerian Laser Power in his mind. The effect was immediate. A laser beam extruded from his paw and hit the head of the spider, making it explode like white-hot lava. The explosion knocked the hawk out of its jaws onto the ground. However, it quickly recovered and flew up again. The lava, in the meantime, turned into snowflakes and eventually disappeared. The sky brightened as soon as the creature vanished, and a fresh, gentle zephyr started blowing.

"Meow ho! Yay!" shouted the kittens joyfully. "It worked, it worked!"

"Well done, Goldie!" shouted Mawgix, from the hawk. Seabreeze, Clawcia and Melowflues waved at them happily.

"FEISHA, NO!" shouted King Koresque, as he approached the opposite end of the clearing. His favourite, pet monster was dead and gone. Rage surged through him. "ATTACK THEM! SPARE NO ONE," he shouted as he charged on his enormous scorpion. The hundreds of mole-rats screeched and started hurling weapons while running towards them. A parabolic shower of arrows, spears, spiked spheres and ugly, sting beetles flew towards them. On a whim Kattie thought of jumping out of the way, and viola, the entire group leaped into a higher plane, out of reach of the weapons. The metallic weapons fell to the ground, having made no contact. This even shocked Kattie.

"What just happened?" asked Tufty.

"I think I just found my personal power. I can make gigantic leaps under the influence of the Core Fulcrum. Not only I but my whole group."

They felt thrilled for her.

The sea of sting beetles, however, changed their paths and swarmed higher towards them. In the meantime, under them, a lot of the mole-rat guards turned into frozen statues, thanks to the ultraviolet-lavender-freeze guns wielded by Mawgix and Seabreeze. Many of the others got stuck on the ground, thanks to the shots from Billy, Clawcia and Melowflues. None of the weapons impacted the king as the special barrier seemed to protect him. Goldie removed the UAC from his bag and targeted one sting beetle, in his mind thinking of the entire swarm. The laser beam hit one bug, and like a web, the laser beam connected with all the other bugs. They suddenly stopped in midair, confused about what to do. He then spoke into the microphone, asking them to attack the mole-rats instead. Promptly, they turned around and zoomed towards the mole-rats to sting them. The mole-rats, seeing the changed state of affairs, abandoned all their weapons and ran in the opposite direction. They could not reach very far however, before the bugs stung them badly and made them collapse.

"Goldie! You found your power! You can control an entire group of animals in one shot!" shouted Snowball.

It stunned Goldie when he realised this. He couldn't wait to find out what Snowball and Tufty's personal power was. The king, upset about his reduced battalion, released his prime weapon, the poison-dart dandelion. The dandelion spun high in the air towards them and released thousands of poisoned darts that took aim at them. Goldie could not use the UAC on them since they were not living. Just as they closed in on the kittens, Snowball threw the special silver dust around them in the hope they would rise further. However, the dust came in contact with the metallic, poisoned darts, and converted them into actual, natural dandelions! The converted dandelions now fell softly around them, leaving them unharmed. Snowball had found his individual power.

At the same moment, the kittens saw another falcon swoop into the clearing. Professor Inabaox, Kusti and Kedi were in it. They performed a mental hurray as soon as they saw them. King Koresque knew this was the time to introduce his ace. He sat on the sting of the scorpion that raised him to the level of the group with the cube. The kittens targeted their claws and weapons at him, but they just bounced off the hard armour. King Koresque cackled evilly.

"Don't even think about it! You may have destroyed my army, but you have still lost, because I HAVE THE PIVOT!" he said and removed the black stone from his cloak. As he raised the stone with both his hands above his head, all the surrounding light specs whirled around him and got absorbed in the stone, turning the star dust into ash. It horrified the kittens to think they would lose the cube after they fought so gallantly for it. They would lose all their powers in a few seconds. Kattie felt tears glisten in her eyes. The ones in the hawk looked dejected too.

Professor Inabaox, however, looked amused. Snowball looked at him, shocked that he found the situation funny. The king too thought it was strange, and his smile vanished.

"You—silly mole-rat bandicoot! That is not the real pivot. No one has found the real one yet. The search continues till

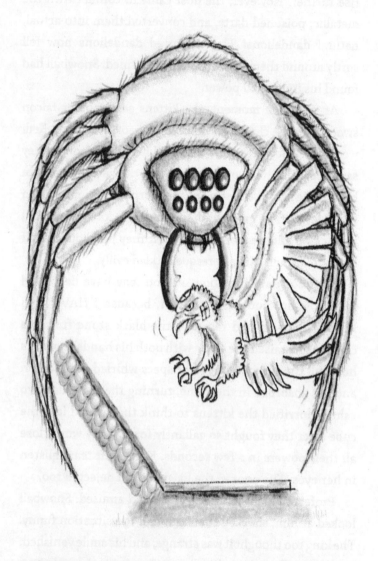

The gigantic spider captures the hawk in its chelicerae

date. Some of us even think it's an urban legend. The one you hold is a miniature replica -- an artist's imagination," said Professor Inabaox, with a devilish glint in his eye.

"You lie! Can't you see it turning light into ash?"

"Yes, the miniatures can turn dust into ash, but has no impact on the Core Fulcrum. It like the difference between a sneeze and a hurricane. A tissue sheet can absorb a sneeze, but can it a hurricane?"

After absorbing all the light specs in its vicinity, the black stone's effect subsided as the professor mentioned. The radiance from the Core Fulcrum grew brighter, illuminating everything around it.

"Aargh!" said the infuriated King, as he threw the black stone far away into the forest.

Professor Inabaox aimed his paw at the scorpion, converting it into a real one. The scorpion, angry at having to carry the weight of a large mole-rat bandicoot, raised its sting. The king jumped down and bounded off into the forest, with it hot in his pursuit. The remaining mole-rats fled the battleground too. All the felids laughed with relief.

Kattie used her powers to bring the group back to ground level, along with the cube. Professor Inabaox, Kusti and Kedi patted all of them and hailed them for their bravery.

"Goldie, I saw what you did with the spider. - It was a perfect execution of the Valerian Laser Power. Good job!"

Goldie blushed and beamed. Shortly, Mawgix too made the hawk land next to them, and they spilled out to gush over the brave little kittens. Goldie, Snowball, Tufty and Kattie were immensely grateful to them for backing them up. They hugged all of them gratefully. The cube, radiantly bobbed up and down amidst this happy gathering.

"We should leave now," said Professor Inabaox. "They could be back anytime. Let us depart while the scene is clear."

Professor Inabaox, Kusti and Kedi boarded their falcon once more, taking the cube with them, and it took off into the air. They hovered high above, waiting for the others. Mawgix, Seabreeze, Billy, Clawcia and Melowflues got into the hawk, and this time Seabreeze flew it towards the airborne falcon containing the teachers. Goldie and his gang bounded towards their parked falcon. Goldie agreed to be the pilot for the return journey. Just as he boarded the bus, a twig snapped behind them. Tufty felt the heat rising in his body, an augury of the enemies' presence near them. Ideally, the effect of the Valerian juice should have worn off by then. Which meant, this was Tufty's personal power. It was probably one of the mole-rat bandicoots again. They had no time to lose.

"Board fast, board fast!" shouted Goldie, turning the ignition on. Kattie jumped in over Tufty and Snowball. The falcon took wing with Tufty and Snowball still near the door. With the sudden jolt, Snowball slipped on the steps.

"Tufty help me!" he called out in alarm.

Tufty turned around and got shocked when he saw Snowball hanging from the last step with his left paw. He bent and stretched down as far as he could to heave him up. They were now above the treetops and fast losing ground.

"Grab my paw now, Snowball!" he shouted to Snowball.

Just then, an arrow sailed across the sky and pierced Snowball's right shoulder. He winced in pain but held on. They were flying high over the sea by then. Tufty screamed with urgency while holding his paw out, and Snowball tried to heave himself up. Another arrow struck Snowball on the paw that held the last step. Unable to bear the pain, he let go of the step and fell backwards into the sea, as Tufty watched in horror. Wanting to find an explanation to the commotion at the door, Katie walked to the entrance and screamed. Goldie almost lost control of the falcon when Kattie told him, and he burst into tears. He made the falcon fly low, skimming the waves so they could discern the depths. Professor Inabaox and Mawgix, who had been waiting for Goldie's falcon in the sky, joined him in the search. The arrows and spears continued flying towards them and hitting their crafts. Mawgix took his hawk back to the shore to stop them. After they dealt with the dozen pesky culprits, they returned. The falcons and the hawk scanned the whole area for a long time, but there was no sign of Snowball. Goldie was inconsolable as Kattie hugged him. Snowball was not only his twin brother, but his best friend. Memories of moments spent together constantly flashed before him. Snowball was always full of humour and life. He constantly joked around and pranked others good-humouredly, but Goldie chided him frequently. Now he regretted it.

"I will send an underwater search party for him, but we must return now," said Professor Inabaox, patting him. "Let us not give up on hope."

After a lot of convincing, Goldie finally agreed to return to Mew Scape. The school sent many search parties to look for Snowball via air, land, and water, but they could not find him. The defenders found Trapesky abandoned during their multiple search operations. When they could not trace him even after a month, they held a funeral in his honour, which even Paka and Niamy attended. Goldie found it hard to believe his brother was no more.

Goldie, Kattie, Tufty received golden-level bravery awards in front of the whole school from both Professor Quemarke and President Skailimet. Mawgix, Seabreeze, Clawcia, Melowflues and Billy received silver bravery awards. They telecasted this award ceremony on prime television all over Eartavista. As he accepted the award, Goldie kept thinking about Snowball. Without his presence, the rescue operation would have been futile and unsuccessful. He deserved this award too. After his demise, Goldie's thoughts only centred around King Koresque's iniquity. They needed to capture the rogue king to prevent the destruction of Eartavista. The defenders who returned from search expeditions could not locate the mole-rats, which meant they had moved to another county. Professor Quemarke recruited the courageous fifth-graders as Defenders. Since he was now part of the Defender program, he would train harder and return to hunt for King Koresque.

The day that Professor Inabaox brought the cube back, he took it to school. Professor Quemarke and President Skailimet met him in the Crystal Cavern. They walked along the passages until they entered the labyrinth. After that, aided by a map held by Professor Inabaox, they walked through it, twisting and turning along its dingy pathways for over an hour. The cube offered ample light as it hovered between Professor Inabaox and President Skailimet. Finally, they reached a large door. President Skailimet and Professor Quemarke had two halves of a key. They joined it to create the shape of a cat sitting on a cube and turned it in the key hole. Their bronze 'Felidae Aurum' pendants glistened even in the dim light.

The door opened into a cylindrical glass passage surrounded by water, where a turtle lay waiting. They sat in the turtle that slid out of the glass passage and dived into the water. Soon it arrived at an underwater glass bubble. A door opened in the bubble to admit the turtle and then closed around them. They got out of it to walk towards another door that led into a well-lit inner glass chamber, fitted with cameras all around. Various colourful fish and sharks swam above and around the weapon-proof bubble. They placed the Core Fulcrum within this chamber where it floated happily. Little did most of the inhabitants of Eartavista know that Purrhy Lake was in the caldera at the centre of the Vistalava volcano. The central island still contained the caves and tree houses that Dr. Diadoms and his group of scientists used for their prehistoric workshops. However, those were not open to tourists.

"An open-air chamber on the island proved too risky, hence I've got this glass chamber built underwater. Although we have exposed the cube to enough light, we placed it fifty feet underwater for its protection. There is a deep glass column under it that connects to the bottom of the lake to provide it with stability. This part of the lake is a private and protected lagoon, so we will have no trespassers too," said Professor Inabaox.

Professor Quemarke and President Skailimet approved. They had financed a new hideout for the cube and had made Professor Inabaox in charge for that operation too. He was proving to be a perfect guardian. Purrhy lake got its possession back, with more robots protecting it than ever before. The two cloaked mole-rats, who had stolen it from its cordoned-off central island, would find it impossible to burrow underwater.

Meanwhile, somewhere, far away from Trapesky, King Koresque was on his way to Vamoush with his hundred-thousand burghers. He vowed to make it the most impenetrable kingdom in the world. Though he had failed to destroy the cube this time, he had not lost hope. The next time, he would surely succeed. In addition, it would be impossible for prisoners to escape alive. Despite all these plans, he felt humiliated by the defeat. He had lost hundreds of his soldiers and Fiesha -- his pet spider because of those felids. Arachnio -- his scorpion had also turned against him. He had no choice but to capture him and lock him in a cage. The king felt Joybob and Trixy were to blame. They had cheated him by bringing him a fake Pivot. Desperately wanting to wring their necks, he had sent a search party for them to all the nearby mole-rat inhabited counties. However, no one could trace them anywhere as they were busy enjoying a vacation with their respective families on a remote beach island on the other side of Eartavista.

* * *